FIC PHILLIPS

D1535039

FEARLESS

NEW YORK TIMES BESTSELLING AUTHOR

Carly Phillips

DATE DUE

MAY 29 2018		
JUN 14 2018		
JUL 12 2018		
JUL 16 2018		
JUL 27 2018		
AUG 28 2018		
SEP 04 2018		
SEP 15 2018		

Discard

PRINTED IN U.S.A.

Copyright © Karen Drogin, CP Publishing 2018
Print Edition
Fearless Cover Photo and Design: Sara Eirew

* * *

All rights reserved. No part of this book may be reproduced in any form by any
means without the prior written consent of the Publisher, excepting brief quotes used
in reviews.

This book is a work of fiction. Names, characters, places, and incidents either are
products of the author's imagination or are used fictitiously. Any resemblance to
actual events or locales or persons, living or dead, is entirely coincidental.

Fall in love with the Wards

Mechanic and garage owner, Kane Harmon is used to the wealthy beautiful women visiting his beach town. He doesn't get involved because he knows most females would merely be slumming for the summer.

Except Halley Ward isn't just passing through. She lives a solitary life in a bungalow on the beach. A woman tormented by her past, distant from her wealthy family, different from Kane's usual fare of town girls who know his M.O.—Don't expect more than he's willing to give.

Kane rescues Halley and her broken down car from the side of the road and instantly he's hooked. She says she's not interested in him. He knows she lies. And he makes it his mission to bring her back to life, to return her emotionally to her family. To show her the colors around her were as vibrant as the ones she puts on her canvas.

Until past meets present and threatens all the progress they've made. Then it's Hayley's turn to step up and stand up for the relationship and life she's finally coming to believe she deserves.

Chapter One

"KANE! PICK UP on Route 5. Lady needs a tow," Kane Harmon's father, Joe, called out from the office in Harmon's Garage.

Kane wiped his greasy hands on a rag and pushed himself out from beneath the jacked-up car he'd been working on. He rose to his feet and glanced around the empty shop, taking stock of his situation. Jackson Traynor, who usually handled the runs with the tow, was out. He'd gone to the city to pick up an emergency part, meaning Kane and his dad, Joe, were the only ones here. Joe, who Kane had no desire to leave by himself.

Temptation was always too great for Kane's father. If he could pocket something to pawn, trade, or sell for extra cash, he'd do it to fuel his gambling addiction. Unfortunately Kane couldn't send his dad out on the run because the older man was no longer allowed to drive. Too many accidents and he'd had his license revoked.

But Kane wasn't going to leave a woman stranded on the highway, so he'd have to go take care of the tow himself. He headed for the office and found his father sitting behind the desk, writing on a scrap pad. Kane hoped it wasn't notes on horses or ball games.

"Hey," Kane said, striding around to the back of the desk, coming up behind his father. "I'm going to go do the pickup since Jackson's out." While he spoke, he pulled a key out of his pocket and opened the cash drawer, removing the bills that were in there.

At a glance, there were hundreds, fifties and smaller denominations separated in the till. He didn't leave anything behind to provide his father the least little bit of temptation.

"You've got to be shitting me." His father's eyes were on the money Kane shoved into his front pockets. "You don't trust me," he said sullenly.

"No, Dad, I don't. Why should I?"

There'd been holiday money he'd gambled away when they were kids, and when things were bad, his dad's motto was, *If it isn't nailed down, it's fair game.* Kane didn't feel the least bit guilty doing what he had to do to make sure he could provide for the family when his father couldn't. Joe wouldn't steal while Kane was in the shop. Kane knew that. It was only when nobody was around to see or answer to that the demon on his shoulder got the best of him and temptation took over.

His dad muttered something under his breath, undecipherable but obviously mean, and Kane chose to ignore him.

"I shouldn't be gone long. Hold down the fort?" Kane asked.

"Oh. You'll trust me to talk to customers?" Sarcasm dripped from his dad's words. "Last time I looked, it was my name on the signage," he muttered.

And last time Kane checked, he was the one running the business. True, the building was in his father's name, but the old man wouldn't budge on adding Kane or his older sister to the deed. The only salvation was the fact that Joe knew his limitations. He'd given Kane ownership of the business when he turned twenty-two, after a bad run with some loan sharks. Kane stepped in and paid off the debt, and in exchange, the business was in Kane's name. Just not the land. Kane wanted it divided between himself and Andi, but his father's pride demanded he hold on to it until he passed on. Which, thank God, didn't look like it would be any time soon.

His father drove Kane mad but he loved his old man. Joe had raised them since his mom died from ovarian cancer when Kane was fifteen and had done the best he could with the limited skill set he had. His heart was in the right place even if his vices weren't.

Kane palmed the truck keys in his hands. "Don't forget Nicky's coming by after day camp," he reminded his dad.

His sister Andrea's seven-year-old son spent afternoons at the garage with his uncle and grandfather while his mom worked. With Nicky's father out of his life—and good riddance—it was important for Nicky to spend time with the men in his family. Not to mention it freed his sister up to work and not worry about her kid after school or summer camp, which saved her from having to hire a sitter. And Kane liked having his nephew around. Even if he was under a car, Nicky did his homework or played games on his cell phone in the office and chatted up his grandpa. It was good.

Kane stepped into the blazing, late-afternoon sunshine, appreciating the summer heat on his face. Once he was outside, he forgot about the aggravation with his dad and instead inhaled the fresh air after being cooped under a car for the better part of the day.

He slid his aviators on his face and climbed into the flatbed, starting up the engine. He drove out of town and onto the highway, music blasting on the radio, until he caught sight of the gleaming, bright red Ford SUV on the side of the road.

The influx of summer visitors into Rosewood Bay,

his ocean-side town in New England, usually meant expensive foreign cars littering the side of the main street and taking up the prime parking near the beach. This little beauty didn't strike him as one of those, but he didn't recognize it as one of his regulars, either.

He pulled in behind the SUV onto the shoulder of the road and parked. After hopping out, he strode to the front of his vehicle and saw a woman in a flirty dress bent over the open hatch as she draped what looked like a sheet over something in the far back.

He shoved his hands into the front pockets of his jeans and looked his fill of the sweet ass aimed in the air and long legs leaning against the edge of the back, his dick perking up and taking notice. Which was a refreshing change, since he no longer partook of the women who came to Rosewood during the summers, willing to indulge in a fun fling with a mechanic but never, ever deigning to consider him good enough for anything more. Once burned, and all that. Actually, it'd been too damn long since he'd been with any woman and even longer since one had truly interested him.

Before he could make his presence known, though she had to have heard his truck's arrival, she turned around and met his gaze.

Recognition slammed into him, raw and real. "Halley Ward," he muttered. "Well, I'll be damned." The girl he knew not at all but had protected from bullying back in high school stood before him, all grown up.

"Hi, Kane," she said softly, shading her eyes from the sun with her hands. Eyes he knew were a light blue.

She'd been quiet and withdrawn back then, head almost always hidden inside a hooded sweatshirt, only her two long braids hanging out from her protective armor. But he knew her story.

Everyone did.

This town thrived on gossip, and the Wards provided much of it over the years. In Halley's case, everyone knew she'd been rescued from foster care at thirteen by her aunt but never seemed to adjust to life back home with her wealthy family. She didn't reach out to other girls or make friends at school or in town. Or maybe they didn't welcome her. He hadn't been sure.

He'd only known that, at the time, he had recently lost his mom and pulled back from the world, so he recognized that same sense of sadness and loss in Halley and had stepped in when the kids gave her a rough time because of her past. They'd never talked or bonded, but he knew she appreciated his efforts. Could tell by the lingering, sad but grateful looks she passed him in the hall that his actions meant something to her.

Despite living in the same town, he hadn't seen her

in years. That damned gossip indicated she was more reclusive and damned more solitary than he was. She didn't hang out at the Blue Wall, the main bar in Rosewood, on Friday or Saturday nights, at least not when he'd been there. Had he wondered more about her through the years? Sure. But life went on.

"So. Dead SUV?" he asked, gesturing to her ride.

"Dead SUV," she said, sounding pissed off. "What kind of car just... dies? It's not new but it isn't ancient, either." She braced her hands on her slender hips and frowned at her vehicle.

He shrugged. "Won't know until I get it jacked up and take a look." He met her gaze. "How've you been?" he asked.

"Good." She toyed with a strand of hair.

With the sun streaming down, he took in those brown locks with sun-kissed streaks of blonde closer to the ends that hung just past her shoulders. And he immediately noticed that the face she'd hidden as a kid was all the more striking now.

Seriously.

She was fucking beautiful. And still fragile at least in appearance, her skin like porcelain, her features delicate, with a hint of freckles over the bridge of her nose. And there was still that whisper of sadness that fell over her features, there whether she was aware of it or not.

"You?" she asked. "How are you? Still working at the garage, I see?"

He'd had a job there from the time he was a kid, hanging out from a young age, just as Nicky did now.

Kane nodded. "I own the place." He wasn't sure why he felt compelled to let her know.

"That's good." She ran her hands up and down her arms.

"Let me get your truck on the flatbed and we'll go back to the garage. I'll take a quick look and see if I can tell you what we're dealing with."

"Thanks."

"You're welcome to hang out in the front of the cab while I work," he said.

She smiled. "And thanks again." She spun on her low-heeled sandals, and her floral dress, which clung to her curves, spun out around her thighs.

Flirty. Cute. Sexy as fuck.

He did his thing and soon they were on their way back to the garage. "So what's covered in the back of your truck?" he asked, having seen the sheet for himself.

"Paintings. I paint. My work is in the gallery in town. I was taking a few pieces over when my car died and I didn't want the sun beating down and fading them."

"An artist? Damn. I'll have to stop by the place

and see your work." He was impressed with that little bit of knowledge about her.

His hands on the wheel, he glanced over. A blush stained her cheeks. "I'm not sure my work is your style."

"Doesn't mean I don't want to see it anyway. Besides, how would you know what my style is?"

"You're right. I don't," she murmured. She curled her hands around her purse on her lap and he refocused on the road.

"Maybe we could change that." Now where had that suggestion come from?

Her gaze swung to his. Startled. "What are you saying?"

"Go out with me sometime." No, he hadn't planned it, but Halley Ward intrigued him. She always had. And now that they were adults, she fascinated him even more.

"I don't date." That surprised him… but it shouldn't, now that he gave it some thought.

It wasn't like he saw her out and about anyway, and she did like to keep to herself. But not to even date? What was that all about?

"Then call it two old friends catching up," he said, now even more determined to find out.

He glanced over to find her lips twitching in amusement she was obviously trying not to show. She might not *want* to be interested in going out with him... but she was.

"We weren't friends," she reminded him gently.

"Do friends stand up for each other?" he asked.

She nodded. "They do."

"Then I'd consider us friends." He looked at her and winked. "Just think about it," he said as he pulled into the garage lot.

Because he was definitely interested in her. Maybe it was fate that her car broke down and he'd been the one to answer the call, bringing them together again after all these years. They were adults now, and he wanted to get to know what secrets she held behind those blue eyes.

Because he sensed, then and now, that her layers ran deep. And he wanted to peel them back and learn what lay beneath.

HALLEY JUMPED FROM the truck and walked around to where Kane stood. She hadn't seen him since high school, and his impact on her hadn't lessened, merely grown.

He'd been a brooder, much like her in male form, except people liked him, unlike her. She hadn't transitioned well from foster care to living in this small coastal town with her aunt. She hadn't wanted any part of it or the kids here, and they hadn't welcomed her in return. But Kane had been her protector, her silent hero, and she'd always been grateful.

She never knew why he'd decided to look after her when the others made her a target with name calling, stuffing her locker with trash... and they'd never talked about it... or anything else, for that matter. They hadn't been friends, as she'd said to him earlier. Oddly they hadn't not been friends, either. They'd just gone their own way.

And yet here they were. He was working on her car and asking her out.

"Listen, if you want to go wait in the office, I'll take a look at your truck. See if I can get you a quick, easy answer or if it's something that's going to take more time," Kane said.

She met his stare, that deep brown gaze staring back at her. Dark hair, grown out, fell over his eyes, giving him an edgy, sexy look. Then there was his body. Muscles showing thanks to his tight black tee shirt, faded jeans molding to strong thighs and a tight ass she'd noticed before.

She sighed. If she dated, she'd go out with him. But she didn't date because it led to relationships, and relationships led to sharing and men asking questions about her past. And she didn't like to go there, to think about foster care or the things that had happened there.

She walked into the office he'd pointed out earlier and came to an abrupt halt. A young boy sat at the desk doing something on his phone, and that was a sight she hadn't expected to find.

"Hi there," she said to the top of his brown hair.

"Hey." He looked up, pencil in hand.

"I'm Halley," she said. "Who are you?"

"Nicky."

Oh. That wasn't at all enlightening. She sat down on the chair near the desk. "I'm just waiting for Kane to check out my car," she said to the boy.

"Cool. Uncle Kane knows cars."

"I'll bet he does," she murmured. She bet Kane knew a lot of things. Like how to make a girl burn with those calloused, grease-stained hands of his. She definitely had visions of him running them over her body, her breasts, her hips and—She shook her head and guided her mind to more appropriate topics.

She realized Nicky had just given her some more information, an inkling to whom he belonged. She recalled Kane having a sister and they'd all been fairly close in age. If he was Uncle Kane, Nicky was Andrea's child.

"Nicky, your mom's here," a male voice called. A second later, an older gentleman walked into the room.

From the look of him, he was definitely Kane's

father, the similarity in their features unmistakable. And if this was what Kane would look like when he aged, he'd continue to be extremely good-looking, she mused. The Harmons had excellent genes.

"Hello there," he said to Halley.

She rose to her feet. "Hi. Halley Ward," she said, extending her hand.

"Joe Harmon," he said, shaking it in greeting. "Nice to meet you. You must be the tow Kane just brought in."

She nodded. "That would be me."

"Well, we'll get you sorted and out of here quickly. In the meantime, feel free to relax. There's a soda machine right inside the garage if you're so inclined," he said.

"Thank you."

"Nicky? Let me walk you out to your mom. She's in a rush and can't come in today."

"Okay, Grandpa." The boy gathered his camp bag and shoved his phone into a gray backpack. Then he came out from behind the desk, all long limbs and the Harmon family dark hair.

Joe Harmon walked his grandson out front, and through the window, Halley watched him climb into an SUV. She couldn't see the woman in the front seat because of the glare of the sun. With a shrug, she turned back.

She picked up her purse from the floor and dug through it for some dollar bills before heading into the garage for a cold soda. She returned and settled back into the chair, popping the top on the can and taking a long sip.

She tapped her foot, waiting, hoping for good news about her car. Her Aunt Joy had bought her the SUV, used because she'd known Halley wouldn't want to accept something extravagant. She'd already bought her the beach house. Because Aunt Joy was trying to buy Halley. Not in a bad way, either. It was just the only way someone with money, who wanted things to be good, easy, normal between them, knew how to act. And what was Halley supposed to do but graciously accept and try to be what Joy wanted?

But Halley didn't feel normal. She didn't feel like everyone else. Life had been hard for her, and she hung on to the pain because it was all she'd known, at least until she was thirteen and Aunt Joy had shown up and saved her from her last foster home, where she'd landed after the trauma with the Smiths. There, the worst hadn't happened, but bad things had. And though Halley knew she ought to be grateful to her aunt and she was, the child in her just wished Joy had found her and Phoebe sooner.

She didn't mean to make Aunt Joy pay for something out of her control. She just didn't know how to be any way but what she was. She was a loner by nature. And Aunt Joy and Halley's older sister, Phoebe, weren't. Halley didn't want to think about this anymore.

She looked around the garage, the beat-up beige walls, the toy cars and trucks on the shelves, a half-dead plant on another. Joe hadn't returned, she realized. And she continued to tap her foot.

The trill of her phone rang from her bag, giving her something to do. She dug it out and saw Phoebe was calling. She answered, wondering what her sister, who was usually busy showing houses as a Realtor to the wealthy, wanted.

"Hello?"

"Hi, Halley! Guess what?" Phoebe asked.

"What?" she asked because she really had no idea.

"I sold the old Callahan Estate!" she said of the massive mansion on the outskirts of town that had been empty since its owner, an elderly woman, passed away five years ago. The heirs had been ridiculous in their demands on price, at least according to Phoebe, and so the place had sat vacant.

"That's fantastic!" Halley said, happy for her sister. "That's a huge coup!" Not only a financial windfall, but Phoebe had managed something her competitive fellow agents hadn't been able to do.

"Thank you. We're going out to celebrate. Dinner

and drinks at the Blue Wall. Aunt Joy said she'd watch Jamie," she said of her son, who was eleven years old.

"Wait. What?" Her mind flew back to what her sister had just said. *We're going out.* "I'm not going. Surely you want to celebrate with Nate and the people from your office." She mentioned Phoebe's friend, and anyone else Halley could think of to keep her sister company so she didn't have to join in.

Halley did not want to go out tonight. She never wanted to go out. Especially to the Blue Wall, where, yes, they could have a private dinner on the restaurant side of the establishment, but where they'd inevitably end up on the bar side afterwards. And Halley didn't like big crowds and guys trying too hard to pick her up.

"I'm not—"

"You are. I'll be at your place at seven. I'll drive," her sister said, and Halley recognized that tone in her voice. They might not have grown up together, having been sent to separate foster homes, but they'd been reunited long enough for Halley to realize Phoebe wouldn't take no for an answer.

Halley pushed down the anxiety that followed and said, "Okay. Only because you deserve a celebration." She'd just try and find an excuse to leave right after dinner.

"Good. Dress up," her sister ordered. "Have to go.

Love you, bye."

"Love you, too," Halley muttered to the dial tone.

Despite being pushed into something she didn't want, Halley smiled, happy for her sister.

"Good news?" Kane asked, as she realized he'd walked into the office and had been waiting for her to finish her call.

"My sister sold a house she's excited about."

He grinned and that was a good look on him. "Good for her," he said as he wiped his hands on a rag.

How could a man look so sexy doing something so simple? She wondered, taking in his strong forearms and masculine hands, drinking him in and hoping he didn't notice she just might be ogling him.

"What's up with my car?" she asked, her voice a little rough. She hoped for some positive news of her own.

"The fuel pump is out. I need to order a new one. I called, and unfortunately it's going to take a few days, probably through the weekend." He shot her a regret-filled look.

She sighed. "Okay, well, thanks for taking care of it. I'll call my sister for a ride home."

"I can take you," he said, catching her off guard.

She shook her head. "You really don't have to go out of your way."

He lifted a shoulder in a lazy shrug. "I don't mind. Let me just go upstairs, wash up, and we can get going."

"Upstairs?"

"I live in the apartment over the garage," he explained. "I'll be right back."

"Umm, okay," she said, agreeing to something she didn't think she wanted for the second time in a few minutes.

But that was a lie. Because as she watched Kane stride out of the office, his muscular yet lean body a sight she couldn't ignore, she realized, for the first time in forever, she desired something.

She desired Kane Harmon.

Chapter Two

K ANE DROVE HALLEY to her house on the beach. He didn't need directions until they got closer, since he didn't know exactly where she lived. She was quiet on the trip over and he let her be, mostly because he didn't plan to just drop her off and walk away. He had, while upstairs washing up, thought quite a bit about this enigmatic woman and whether he wanted to put in the effort to pursue her.

He normally didn't have to work hard to get a female into his bed. Not that he was bragging, but ever since he'd been aware of his interest in the opposite sex, they'd come easily and willingly. He hadn't had many long-term relationships, mostly because no one woman had held his interest for long, but he wanted to get involved with someone who could be with him for the long haul. His parents had had a good marriage despite his father's failings. His mom had put up with the gambling, probably because it hadn't been as bad when she was alive to keep him in check. And though Kane hadn't met the right person, he'd like to.

Of course, he was plenty busy with his family, keeping his father on the straight and narrow and keeping an eye on his sister's kid when he could.

Once he arrived at Halley's cottage, which was a name many houses in this area had, he realized it was a misnomer. He took in the beautiful structure, the water lapping in the background, the gorgeous porch in the front, and the visible wraparound deck in the back, and he was struck with the enormity of Halley's family's wealth.

It didn't bother him, not in the way of *she's out of my league*. Which was odd, considering ever since Liza had slept with him, led him to believe she was interested in a relationship only to dump him when her summer at the beach ended, with her amused comment that he'd believe she'd remain involved with a mechanic, of all things, he avoided the women who vacationed here during the season. Women who rented the type of house Halley lived in for the hot months of July and August. But nothing about Halley screamed standoff-ishness because of either her money or family status, so he immediately put it out of his mind.

Nothing really mattered but chemistry and the genuineness of a person, or so he believed, something he'd never found in the summer visitors. But Halley, for all her wariness about people, was as genuine as they came. No airs. So yeah, he'd decided, though he didn't know her well, he wanted to go for the pursuit.

He parked the car he drove, a classic royal-blue Camaro, and climbed out, determined to beat or at least meet her around by her side.

She'd already swung her legs out and stood, glancing at him with a confused expression on her pretty face. "What are you doing?"

"Walking you to your door," he said with his most charming smile on his face.

"But... this isn't a date. You're dropping me off after doing me a favor."

"Aah. But my father raised a gentleman, and a gentleman always walks a lady to her door."

She shot him a skeptical glance. She was on guard, as she should be, because he wasn't planning to leave her on her front porch and walk away. Not if he could help it.

"Your house is gorgeous. Have you lived here long?" he asked as they walked up the gravel drive and along the well-gardened, cultivated path leading to the door.

"Yes. And no." She hesitated, then said, "My aunt bought the house five years ago, while I was living with my sister in the guest cottage on the property of the family's main house."

She didn't elaborate on where that was. Everyone in Rosewood knew of the Ward Estate and she obviously knew it.

"So you moved in then?" he asked.

She shook her head. "For a while I used it as a painting studio. I figured my aunt would rent it out, but she insisted the place was mine. I wasn't exactly comfortable accepting a house as a gift." She shrugged awkwardly. "But the view and the peacefulness for my work, well, they couldn't be beat. I spent more and more time here painting, sometimes staying overnight. Eventually I just moved in." She blushed, obviously uncomfortable.

He understood. Who gave this kind of expensive house as a gift? It was beyond generous. He sensed there was more to the story with her aunt that he wouldn't be getting from her now.

She pulled her keys from her purse, deliberately dangling them in front of him. "I'm here."

And you can go now. He heard the unspoken words and grinned. "I was kind of hoping for a tour of the place."

She rolled her eyes at him in a gesture he found cute. "Kane, this is a small... ish," she conceded, "Cottage on the beach. There's nothing to see."

"Except the view from the back," he corrected her. "I love the water. I'd like to see."

He wasn't backing down. If he lost this battle, he'd lose the war. She'd push him away; he'd drive off and lose ground. Not happening.

"Fine," she said in light of his persistence. She unlocked the door and let them inside.

He stepped over the threshold. For the décor, she had minimal beige furnishings. The walls were also a cream with light blue molding and accents, and he could see from the front entrance straight through to wall-to-wall windows with the ocean in the background. The view was spectacular. No wonder she found this a perfect place to paint.

He crossed through the house and stood by the glass, looking out at the gorgeous scenery, the lapping waves and beach beyond. "You're damn lucky to live here," he said. "Can I take a look out back?"

"Sure." She unlocked the slider and they stepped out onto the deck. "Steer clear of that side," she said, pointing to the right, where the deck seemed to fall off midway through.

There were stairs but no railing to help her down, but at least she could easily get to the beach, with its clean sand below and the lapping water hitting the shore. If this were his place, he'd spend most of his time out back. From the looks of the beautiful barbeque grill gleaming in the sunlight on the far side of the deck that was finished, that had been her plan.

"What happened? Are you mid-construction?" he asked.

She came up beside him. "It turns out that the deck was rotting underneath and I had to have it torn down. The guy I hired to do the work building the new one wasn't reliable. He didn't show up on time, sometimes he didn't come at all, or he'd leave early. The supplies were purchased and are under that tarp."

She pointed to the dark, heavy plastic covering what was probably lumber and other materials.

She shrugged. "I haven't had a chance to make phone calls and try to find someone else reliable to finish the job."

He shoved his hands into his pockets and studied the half-finished project. "It's a shame when people can't run a business," he muttered, frustrated on her behalf. He did all the handiwork at his father's place and enjoyed that kind of work in his spare time. This looked like a big job.

"I have a list of contractors. I just have to dig in and actually make the calls."

She started to head back into the house and he took her cue, following her inside, his gaze on the graceful way she walked, the subtle sway of her hips, and the flirty way her dress floated against her legs. Beautiful long legs he could envision wrapped around his hips. He adjusted his pants and bit back a groan.

She shut the door and locked it again, turning back to face him. "So that was the deck and the back. As for the rest of this place, it's a normal house. So now that you've seen it…"

"You'd like me to leave. I got the message." He shoved his hands into his front pockets. "I'll tell you what. I'll go if you agree to one date."

She sighed, her pretty lips pursing. "Kane, don't make me turn you down again."

"I'm persistent. One of these days, you'll say yes." He was sure of it.

An unwilling smile pulled at her lips. "Arrogant much?" she asked.

"Just certain. Because I intend to keep asking, and at some point, you won't be able to turn me down."

She shook her head along with treating him to an eye roll, as if the suggestion was insane. "We went over seven years without running into each other. What makes you think you'll see me again so you can keep asking?"

He winked at her, the answer obvious. "Because now I know where you live and I have your SUV. Good-bye, Halley," he said with a grin. She was a challenge and he didn't mind at all.

He treated her to a raised hand, his version of a wave so-long, and headed for the door, leaving her open-mouthed and speechless.

Just as he'd planned.

✧　✧　✧

THE BLUE WALL was the main restaurant in town. Upscale on one side, where you would go on a date or for a nice dinner, and a bar with live music some nights on the other. The walls were, of course, an aqua blue to match the ocean, and inside the restaurant, there was an enormous fish tank that was spectacular.

Halley sat with her sister in the restaurant, having polished off a delicious lobster dinner, and was now tackling dessert.

"You know I'm proud of you, right?" Halley asked. "I mean, you sold a house nobody else could. You're a goddess."

Phoebe beamed, dressed every inch the successful business woman. Her long white-blonde hair was pulled back in a sleek, low ponytail, and she still wore the cream-colored suit from her earlier home showing. They were sisters, but they looked nothing alike. According to their aunt Joy, they each favored a different parent. Neither Halley nor Phoebe remembered much of what their mother looked like, and their dad had been in the army, deployed to Iraq and killed in action when Halley was three.

"I am a goddess, aren't I?"

"An arrogant one." Halley laughed. "But I love

you."

"And I love you."

They said it often, making up for lost time.

Phoebe raised her champagne glass and took a sip.

And Halley dug into her dessert. Called Fire and Ice, it was vanilla ice cream and mixed heated berries, with a sugary crust on top.

"This is delicious." She slid the spoon into her mouth again, savoring the sweet and tart mix, moaning at the taste. She had a sweet tooth and she was in heaven. "I'm glad you dragged me out tonight for this alone."

Phoebe waved her spoon at Halley. "You know what your problem is?"

"No, but why am I sure you're going to tell me?"

Phoebe grinned. "You don't give things a chance. You stay holed up in your ivory tower—"

"House on the beach," Halley corrected her.

"And you assume you're going to hate every new experience."

"Untrue. I'm trying to get my work out into the world." She wanted one of the bigger Manhattan galleries to pick up her paintings.

She didn't want to do showings where she had to be present, that went against who she was, but she wanted to make real money selling her paintings. She could only charge what people deemed they were worth, and right now she made enough for expenses. She wanted more. Unfortunately, she felt like she'd hit a wall with her latest work, and she wasn't sure what was wrong. Or how to change it.

"That's your work you want out there. Not you. But…" Her sister's expression softened. "You're good. Your time will come."

"I hope so." Gallery owners visited their beach town in the summers and frequented Glaziers Galleries, where Halley showed her paintings. She just needed the right piece to catch the right person's eye.

"I know so," Phoebe said. "But back to my point. Tonight proves you're wrong. New experiences are good for you. You should be more open-minded."

Halley glanced down at her dessert bowl. "Because I liked the ice cream, you've decided I'll like every new experience?" she asked.

Phoebe rolled her eyes.

If they were kids, Halley thought she'd have stuck out her tongue. But she couldn't really know what Phoebe would have done when they were children. They'd been separated and sent to different foster homes. Halley had been all of three. Phoebe had been six. And Juliette, she'd been all of two years old when her real father, a different parent than Halley and Phoebe's dad, had taken her away for good. Their *loving* mother had all but sold Juliette to her biological father in exchange for cash to support her drinking and drug habit, and when the neighbors reported her for neglect, Halley and Phoebe had been taken away next.

Halley shook her head and shivered at her thoughts. Most of that information had been passed on by their aunt in a kinder manner than Halley transposed in her own mind.

"Halley!"

Phoebe snapped her fingers and Halley returned to the present. God, why did her thoughts *still* travel back to the awful past?

"Where were you?" her sister asked gently.

Halley swallowed hard. "Nowhere important." But it was time to go home, maybe paint a little and get lost in her work. She already knew sleep wouldn't come easily, if at all.

"Honey—"

She shook her head. "No, it's fine. I'm fine." She didn't want to get into a discussion about her thoughts with her sister.

Phoebe studied her for a long moment, as if assessing what she wanted to say. "Let me get the check and we'll go next door for a drink or two." She met Halley's gaze, her narrowed green eyes daring her to object.

"Yes, I know you were just about to say you wanted to go home. Not happening. This is my celebration and we aren't finished having fun."

With a sigh, Halley took the final scoop of the dessert, savoring her last bit of enjoyment for the evening.

✧   ✧   ✧

KANE WATCHED HALLEY slip a spoon into her mouth, close her eyes, and savor whatever dessert she was eating with relish. In a halter dress with pastel flowers, she stood out in the room. Her lips closed over the spoon, and he could almost hear her moan of delight. His dick hardened in his pants at both the sight and the direction his imagination took him. Halley, with those glossed lips, pulling him into her mouth and sucking. Deep.

He swallowed a groan and forced himself to remember where he was, and why. His sister, Andrea, worked as a hostess at the Blue Wall on weekend nights, and when Kane hit the bar, he stopped by to say hello. Seeing Halley here was a shock. Twice in one day after a long drought—he took that as a sign telling him not to give up despite her reluctance to go out with him. She didn't see him and he kept in the shadows. As he'd told Halley, he knew where to find her now.

"Andi!" he said to his sister, who had just returned to the front of the restaurant. She was dressed in a black skirt and a button-down white lace top, holding menus in her hand.

"Hello, Kane. How's my brother?" She kissed his cheek. "Here for a few drinks and some fun?"

"Actually I'm a man on a mission."

She placed a set of menus beneath the hostess stand. "Really." She studied him through a narrowed gaze. "Who is she?"

He leaned on the wooden podium. "She's interesting and unique. And she paints," he said, knowing he was giving Andi nonsensical information. But she was female. She'd understand he was making a point. The woman on his mind wasn't someone that he'd consider a one-night stand.

"You have a crush on someone. More than a crush, you're really interested. Who is she?" Andi's brown eyes twinkled with enjoyment.

He tapped her nose. "That is none of your business."

She stepped toward him with a sigh and tucked a strand of her brown hair behind her ear. "I'll find out eventually."

"I'm sure you will." When he was ready for her to know. After he'd made progress.

"Good luck," she said, patting his cheek.

He'd need it. He doubted he'd see Halley at the bar, so he'd need to plan his next step.

Except he was wrong. He was on his second beer, shooting the shit with Paul Carver, an old friend, when she walked in alongside her sister. Paul whistled. "Who is that?" he asked, his head tracking the women as they headed toward the other side of the bar.

"Which one are you looking at?" Kane asked, curling his hand into a fist, growing quickly possessive of the woman who had already left an indelible mark on him.

"The gorgeous blonde, of course."

Kane relaxed, the tension in his shoulders easing. "Good. Because I'd hate to have to break your jaw," he said, more good-naturedly than he felt with the blood still pumping through his veins.

Paul barked out a laugh. "So you're staking a claim on the other one?"

"Already staked, my man."

"What do you say to a dual approach?"

Kane placed his beer on the bar counter and inclined his head. "Let's go."

HALLEY'S INSIDES SHOOK as she stood at the bar. She didn't do big rooms of people well, something she'd learned once she returned home as a teenager. She didn't like strangers in her space, standing too close. And after the foster care situations she'd lived through, that made sense and some residual anxiety was understandable.

She picked up her drink and took a sip of her rum and Coke. With a little luck, her sister... and her ride would decide she'd had enough of this scene and decide to go home.

Halley lowered the glass just as a familiar voice said, "That's twice in one day."

She turned and met Kane's gaze. She shouldn't be shocked to see him here. It was the place to go, but she hadn't thought about the fact that she might run into him tonight. And now that she had, her stomach fluttered with butterflies she hadn't felt in... ever.

He'd cleaned up since she'd seen him this afternoon. His hair was still disheveled but in a sexy, just-rolled-out-of-bed sort of way, and he wore a pair of faded denim jeans and a white tee shirt that showed off his muscles the same way as the black one he'd worn this afternoon. She was tempted to squeeze his biceps and see how hard they were beneath her fingers.

She curled her free hand into a ball, her drink still in her other one.

"So tell me. How did I get so lucky?" he asked, his gaze warm on hers.

"My sister wanted to celebrate a big sale." She placed her glass on the bar.

"You mentioned she sold a house earlier."

Halley nodded. "Phoebe is a real estate agent. A pretty amazing one, actually. She sold the Callahan Estate."

He let out a low whistle. "Now that is impressive."

"Right?" She couldn't contain the pride in her voice at her sister's accomplishment. "So we had dinner to celebrate and then she insisted we come here for a few drinks. But…" She gestured to Phoebe, who was now engaged with talking to a good-looking guy with dark hair and a square jaw. "Apparently now she's abandoned me," she said, tongue in cheek.

He laughed. "Then it's a good thing I'm here to step in for her and keep you company."

She couldn't argue with that. Having Kane around was better than standing alone and letting a stranger approach her. "Maybe it is," she murmured.

He raised an eyebrow. "Are you actually happy to see me?" he asked, stepping in closer.

She didn't mind him in her personal space. His masculine scent caused heat to permeate her senses. Her nipples puckered and a rush of wetness coated her panties.

She swallowed hard. "I guess I'm just not into the bar scene."

"And I'm a familiar face," he said, understanding how she was feeling without her having to explain. "I realize we'd left your paintings in the SUV at the garage. Did you want to take them to the gallery?"

She grasped onto the more mundane topic. "I was planning to wait until I get my car back and drop them off then."

Although Faith, who owned the gallery, said she'd prefer to have the paintings before the weekend, Halley might not get them there in time. She could ask Phoebe or Aunt Joy for a ride, but she hated for them to have to go out of their way for her.

"I could take you over tomorrow if you want," Kane offered.

She paused, surprised. "I couldn't put you out."

"It's fine. I can spare the time. In fact, we could get lunch on the way home."

"But—"

"It wouldn't be a date. Just two old friends, one doing the other a favor," he assured her, and she didn't know if she was relieved or disappointed he seemed to have given up on asking her out.

She disliked imposing on people for favors. She still wasn't used to relying on anyone but herself, but Kane seemed to want to help so… "Okay, thank you."

A pleased smile lifted his sexy lips. "Give me your cell. I'll call myself and we'll have each other's numbers. I'll give you a ring before I leave the garage to come by."

She saw the twinkle in his gaze, realized he had an ulterior motive for taking her number, but she found herself digging her cell out of her purse and handing it to him anyway. A few minutes later and they'd each programmed the other's number into their phones.

Kane now had an easy way to reach her. Her stomach fluttered again, something she was getting used to when he was around.

HALLEY LEFT THE bar shortly after talking to Kane. She'd expected to have a hard time sleeping for the usual reasons, because her past left her afraid of the dark, more specifically afraid of passing out and waking up to find someone standing over her. She shivered at the painful memory, but in a surprising turn, that hadn't been the reason for her inability to sleep.

Instead of bad things, her thoughts had been filled with Kane. His sexy smile kept crossing her mind. The way he'd lean in close to her while she was speaking. The curve of his lips when he laughed. The hard muscles in his arms that flexed when he moved. And the appealing smell of him, a warm, heady scent that aroused her senses.

This, she knew, wasn't easy to do. Halley wasn't a woman who threw herself into relationships or casual affairs. She'd been traumatized as a teenager, and though she hadn't been raped, thank God, what she had experienced made her wary of men. So the few times she had found herself wanting company, she'd chosen carefully, made certain it was on her terms.

She didn't date. She had sex. A fling. She'd learned from experience that was the only kind of relationship she was comfortable with having. The type where no one asked anything of her and no attachments were formed. She didn't sleep with or beside anyone, either, because no one needed to know she didn't sleep. Not well and not often. She didn't want anyone asking her why.

Which explained why she put Kane off, why she couldn't say yes to dating him. Because he was a man who'd inevitably want more. And she was afraid he could make her want it, too.

Halley worked through the night, falling into bed around three a.m. She woke up feeling fairly rested considering her lack of sleep. She made herself a cup of coffee and walked out onto the half-finished deck and looked out onto the ocean in the distance.

The sound of waves lapping at the shore reached her ears, soothing her. She breathed in deep, the scent of salt and fresh air filling her nostrils. Kane had seemed to like the view, too, she thought, taking a long sip of her coffee, the sweetened brew helping her to wake up and focus even more.

Her cell, which she'd tossed into her cardigan pocket, rang loudly, startling her. She placed the mug on the floor and pulled her phone out, the caller coming in as blocked.

"Hello?" she asked, wondering who would call her this early in the morning.

Silence greeted her.

"Hello?"

No one answered. She shrugged and disconnected the call.

When the phone rang again, she got annoyed, but a glance at the screen told her it was her sister calling.

"Morning, Phoebe."

"Morning. I'm on my way to work and I just wanted to thank you for coming out last night. I know it's not your idea of fun and it meant a lot to me that you came."

Halley smiled. "I'm glad I did. Your successes deserve to be celebrated."

A beep sounded. "Oops, that's the office. I have to run. Talk to you later," Phoebe said and disconnected the call.

Halley laughed at her always busy sister. She picked up her coffee and headed inside. She wanted to paint before Kane called to pick her up and while the sun was at the perfect angle against the house.

She settled in front of her easel, and what felt like a short time later—but in reality had been a few hours—her phone rang, startling her. The name Kane appeared on the screen and her stomach fluttered accordingly.

"Ridiculous," she muttered as she answered the call. "Hi, Kane," she said.

"Afternoon, Halley. You ready to go drop off your paintings? I loaded them from the back of your SUV into the back of my truck."

She glanced at the canvas she had been working on, the acrylics a brighter color than her past pieces, as she answered.

"I thought you drove that gorgeous Camaro?" The royal blue had gleamed in the sun and the white stripe had been glittering and clean. A gorgeous, sexy car. It suited him.

"I do. But I have the truck for other things. Like driving Nicky around, doing work around my dad's house, grocery shopping, things like that. So your paintings are safe and covered." He cleared his throat. "And beautiful," he said, real admiration in his tone. "Anyway, I'll see you in half an hour if that works?"

"It does. And Kane, thank you." For the compliment, she thought, extremely pleased he liked her work. And for helping her out.

"My pleasure," he said, the words sounding gruff

and meaningful, which she knew was all her imagination. Which, again, was unlike her, reading into what a man said or did. "Plan on stopping for lunch on the way home. There's a place on the beach with the best burgers. Casual and delicious."

Her body tingled with a sudden awareness at the realization that she was going out with Kane. And though her defenses were naturally high, a part of her was looking forward to her afternoon.

Chapter Three

K ANE HELPED HALLEY unload her paintings and carried them into Glaziers. He'd passed by the gallery often, never curious or bothering to go inside. It was funny how he now had a sudden appreciation for art. And the woman painting it.

The gallery owner was a lovely woman in her mid-forties named Faith. She had blonde hair and an affect in her voice, but she was warm and clearly in love with Halley's work, and she, in turn, lit up with the praise. Her cheeks were flushed, and she had an excited note in her voice he hadn't heard from her before. He wanted to see and hear her happiness more often.

Once they finished, they drove to the Shack, his go-to for hamburgers and fries. It was what the name implied, a shack on the beach, a hidden gem in their town.

"Have you eaten here before?" he asked after they'd placed their orders and chosen a small picnic table, the only kind of seating offered here. It was no frills and who he was. Time would tell if Halley approved.

"Nope. But I love a good burger and I'm starving."

She wasn't turning her nose up at his favorite place. That worked for him.

A little while later, they were sitting across from each other. They'd finished their burgers, and Halley was picking at her fries, dipping them in ketchup and delicately placing them in her mouth, one at a time. "Good?" he asked.

She nodded, mouth full, and only after she'd swallowed did she grin. "This place is amazing."

He laughed. "I take Nicky here often. He loves it."

"So he's your sister Andrea's little boy?"

He nodded. "She got pregnant and married Nicky's father. Unfortunately, he wasn't model husband material. He was a deadbeat father who left town, to everyone's relief."

Halley winced.

And Kane's jaw clenched as he told the story, always angry on his sister's behalf. "Andrea hasn't heard from him since. Which, as far as I'm concerned, is a blessing."

"That's awful," Halley murmured.

"Agreed."

"You and your sister are close, aren't you?" she asked.

"Very."

She smiled. "Phoebe and I are close, too, which sometimes surprises me because we're so different."

"How so?" He leaned forward, interested in any glimpse she'd give him into her life.

"Well," she said, twirling a French fry in her hand, "I'm quiet, I like being alone in my house with my painting, and my sister is a people person. That's what makes her so good at her job. She can talk to anyone about anything. With me, it's more like pulling teeth."

He met her gaze. "I like the silent type. It's more intriguing to find out what makes you tick."

She blushed at that. "I'm really not that interesting."

"And I beg to differ." But he wasn't going to push. They'd had a fun lunch, she'd gotten a little comfortable with him, and that was good enough for today.

She took a sip of her soda. "It must be nice working with your dad."

Her topic choice took him off guard. "It's good to have a family business."

"I sometimes wonder what it would be like if my dad had lived," she said, then her eyes opened wide, as if she'd realized what she said.

"What happened to him?"

She looked down. "He was in the army. He died in combat in Iraq."

He reached over and touched her hand. "I'm sorry."

"I was only three. I don't even remember him because he was never home."

She drew her tongue over her lips and he charted the movement, wondering how she'd taste. Sweet? Tart? Would her lips be soft? He couldn't let thoughts of sex distract him from the important fact that she was letting him in, at least a little.

"I lost my mom when I was fifteen," he said, hoping to keep her talking with some truths of his own. "The next few years sucked."

Her eyes grew soft. "That was when you used to help me out in school," she murmured.

"I remember you'd just transferred in and it wasn't easy for you. I had a hard time after Mom died, and I felt like I understood you a little. I wanted to help."

She managed a smile. "You did. More than you can imagine."

"I'm glad."

She glanced at their joined hands, his palm still covering hers. He slid his off her without making an issue.

Then, sensing she'd had enough for one day, he crumpled up the foil wrapper from his burger. "Ready to head home? I need to stop by the garage this afternoon and make sure things are running smoothly."

He'd left Jackson in charge, which wasn't the issue. His father was at the garage, as well. Kane always felt better knowing he'd looked in on his dad.

"Sure," she said, gathering her garbage, too, and they tossed the trash.

They walked side by side to his truck, and he opened her door, helping her up and inside. She was silent on the way home, and it was a comfortable silence, one he didn't take for granted.

Her house wasn't far from the Shack, and they pulled up in front. He jumped out and met her at her side.

She opened her mouth to argue about the need to walk her to the door, but he placed a finger over her parted lips. It was as close as he'd be getting to finding out if they were as soft as he'd imagined.

They were.

"No argument, beautiful."

Once again, that light flush stained her cheeks.

He placed a hand at the small of her back and guided her up the walk to her front door. She turned to face him, eyes wide and... expectant.

He had her off-balance and he liked it that way. She waited for him to speak. Or kiss her, if the look on her face—flushed cheeks, tipped-back head, parted lips—was any indication.

He leaned in and brushed his lips over her cheek. Her skin was even softer than her lips. "Bye, Halley."

"Bye," she whispered as he straightened and walked away. He found it damned hard not to look back.

✧   ✧   ✧

THE NEXT MORNING, a banging noise filtered into Halley's brain, rousing her from sleep. She thought she was imagining it, tried to fall back into the dream she'd been having. A dream about Kane, where the kiss she'd been denied the day before had actually happened. His warm lips had covered hers and his tongue slid over her mouth in a lazy glide, resulting in her letting him inside. She moaned. He gripped the back of her head, tilting her for better, deeper access. His tongue tangled with hers and she hooked a leg around his, arching her hips so her sex ground against his.

The loud banging penetrated her head once more, drumming through her skull, interrupting her recall of the sexy dream.

"Damn," she muttered, forcing her eyelids open and pushing herself up in bed.

The noise sounded like it was coming from the back of the house, and she needed to check out the cause. It was too early on a Sunday morning to be woken out of a sound slumber with hot dreams, especially because she didn't sleep easily and she definitely didn't have sex-filled dreams often, if ever.

She climbed out of bed and retrieved a short silk robe from the back of the chair by the small vanity in her room and pulled it on, knotting the belt at her waist.

Then she walked out of her bedroom and past her easel to the doors leading to the back deck, stopping short at the sight.

Kane had carried a fair amount of the treated wood out from beneath the tarp, and he was in the process of bringing more. Wearing a pair of jeans and a fitted white tee shirt, muscles flexing, he dropped the wood onto the pile, the loud sound explaining the noise.

She was embarrassed now that she knew it was him and he'd interrupted himself starring in her sensual dream. But she needed to know why he was here.

She unlocked the door and flung the slider open. "What's going on?" She tugged on the belt of her robe and stepped outside. "Kane?"

He glanced up, his eyes scanning from her bare feet and legs, up over her body and neck, landing on her face. Pure male approval glittered in his gaze, which, considering she'd just rolled out of bed without checking a mirror, startled her.

He walked over, stopping in front of her. "Good morning."

She swallowed hard and ignored the heat that rushed to her cheeks at his perusal. "Good morning. What are you doing?" she asked him.

"What does it look like I'm doing?" He gestured to the stack of wood he'd accumulated. "I'm fixing your deck."

"Yes, I see that. I meant… why?"

"Because it needs to be done and I like working with my hands."

Her mind raced to the innuendo in that statement, his hands stroking over her body, taking his time, outlining her curves. And when he winked at her, she knew she hadn't been the only one whose mind went *there*.

She cleared her throat. "I appreciate that you want to help me, but I can't take advantage of you like that." *Take advantage.* Jesus. Why did everything out of their mouths feel like it had a sexual connotation?

"You're not taking advantage. I want to do it. I renovated the house my father lives in if you need a reference," he said, and she wasn't sure if he was joking about the referral. "As long as you don't mind me working during my free time, I don't mind getting it done."

"Thank you. Really." She'd have to do what she could to show her appreciation. And very specific ways of giving gratitude came to mind. Her on her knees in front of him, slowly undoing his zipper until his cock sprang free. Gah! What was she doing, thinking about him that way while he watched her, amusement in his knowing gaze?

He reached out and lifted the end of the tie on her robe. "Now that we've settled that, can you do me a favor?" He ran the silk between his thumb and forefinger, slowly. Sensually.

"Of course. Name it," she said in a hoarse croak, mesmerized by the way his calloused fingers caressed the soft material, her nipples hard beneath her camisole.

"Please go put on some damned clothes," he said in a roughened voice. "You're distracting me from my work." His gaze had zeroed in on the hardened peaks poking at her robe.

Oh, God. She blushed, something that was becoming a habit when he was around, turned, and headed inside.

❖   ❖   ❖

KANE HAD BEEN working for a few hours. The morning summer sun grew even hotter against his skin. Halley had brought him cold water a few times, which he appreciated about as much as he did the fact that she'd changed into one of the floaty dresses she preferred, which showed so much of her tanned, bared skin. And thank God she wasn't wearing that short robe that hit her at mid-thigh, teasing him with thoughts of what he'd find if he slid his finger beneath the silk and traveled upward in search of her feminine sex. More than once, he'd nearly hurt himself thanks to the distraction of the woman inside the house.

The sound of a car door slamming distracted him from his thoughts. Another one followed. Halley had company and he wondered who was here. From what he'd gathered so far, she didn't have a big group of friends.

She was so damned interesting to him. It wasn't just the fact that he found her so fucking sexy, or that the desire to taste her everywhere only grew each time they were together. She'd given him a glimpse into the wistful side of herself yesterday, admitting how she wondered if her life would have been different had her father lived. It was a tiny nugget of information, and it opened up more questions than answers, and yet it was something.

An indicator of trust, small though it might be. It was something he could work with.

Build on.

And he intended to use every tool at his disposal. But for now, he needed to get back to work.

✧　　✧　　✧

AFTER LEAVING KANE on the deck, Halley took a shower, painfully aware of the hot man hard at work right outside her house. She rushed through her morning routine, blow-drying her hair and putting on a little makeup, some mascara, foundation, blush, and lip gloss, taking more care than usual because of Kane.

She shouldn't care.

She told herself she didn't. But only a fool would believe those weak protestations. She was too aware of Kane and the heat they generated when they were together. Now he was showing her he was a nice guy, too, something she'd known in the past and now understood hadn't changed.

After Kane had been working for awhile, she took out the ingredients for omelets, intending to make him a meal by way of thanks. Cooking was the only way she could think of to show her appreciation for the hard work he was and would be putting in on her house. She could feed him or send him home with homemade meals so he didn't have to leave here and worry about what he'd eat later.

She was a self-taught cook. She loved watching cooking shows in her free time and creating meals for herself to eat. Considering she didn't go out much, it was her treat to herself and she enjoyed it. Sometimes she invited her sister, nephew, and her aunt over because they worried about how much time she spent holed up painting. This showed them she was fine and they didn't need to be concerned.

She'd taken out everything she needed when her doorbell rang. She looked through the peephole, surprised to see her sister and her aunt standing out front.

She let them in. "What are you guys doing here?" she asked. "Is everything okay?"

"I need to talk to you, and without a car, you can't come to the house," Aunt Joy said, sounding frazzled.

"So we came to you." Phoebe walked into the family room, her gaze immediately going to the noise on the deck. "Is that...?" Her voice trailed off and she stepped closer to the window. "It's Kane Harmon! What's he doing here on a Sunday morning, working on your deck?"

"He—"

"Wait. Didn't I see you talking to him at the Blue Wall on Friday night? Don't tell me you two hooked up?" she asked, her voice lifting, and she sounded hopeful.

Another thing her sister always bemoaned was the fact that Halley didn't go out on dates.

Halley blushed. "What? No! He drove me home from the garage after my SUV died. He saw the house, the unfinished deck, and just showed up to help me out."

Halley glanced at her aunt, who looked on with amusement. She wisely remained silent. She wouldn't gang up on Halley or pump her for information about her private life. That was Phoebe's forte.

"He runs a garage. What does he know about construction?" Phoebe asked.

"He says he's good with his hands," Halley said, folding her arms defensively across her chest. Phoebe would keep prying, she knew.

"I'll just bet he is."

Ignoring her innuendo, which she'd already decided there'd been too much of today, she rerouted the conversation. "So are you guys going to tell me why you're here?"

"It's a long story," her aunt said. "Maybe we should sit."

"I need to put away eggs and milk I took out of the refrigerator first. Come into the kitchen. We can sit in there."

Her aunt nodded and started for the other room.

Phoebe headed after her, pausing by Halley to whisper, "You really need to take advantage of all that male hotness."

Halley rolled her eyes and walked to the kitchen, her sister following.

"Before we get started, do you have anything cold to drink?" Phoebe asked, then, without waiting for an answer, opened the refrigerator to check for herself and pulled out a Diet Coke.

Phoebe often visited and just as often made herself at home. Asking was a courtesy she didn't need to do. "Anyone want one?" she asked.

"No," Halley and her aunt said at once.

Phoebe turned around and met Aunt Joy's gaze.

Halley had the definite feeling she was the only one who didn't know why Aunt Joy needed to talk in person.

"What's going on?" Halley asked, antsy because this felt like an ambush. She couldn't imagine what her aunt needed to discuss that she couldn't do over the phone.

"Let's sit." Aunt Joy walked over to the granite table, one of Halley's favorite things in the house, a mix of black, white, and gray swirls. She pulled out a chair and took a seat, then waited for Halley and Phoebe to join her.

Seated, Halley propped her arms on the table and leaned forward, glancing from her sister to her aunt, struck as she always was by how much they resembled each other in appearance. With their light blonde hair, the women looked like mother and daughter. They shared the straight blonde hair, green eyes, and elegant features. They dressed similarly, too. Where Halley enjoyed loose, flowing dresses and clothing, Phoebe and Joy chose tailored suits and dresses, more fitting for work than a casual day at home. And Joy didn't work. Phoebe's poise also came from their aunt.

Halley looked at them pointedly.

When silence reigned, Halley couldn't wait any longer. "Okay, someone *talk*."

"I had a visitor this morning," Aunt Joy finally said.

"Okay?"

Aunt Joy reached over and took Halley's hand in hers. "My sister... your mother stopped by the house."

She took the words like a punch in the stomach. "What?" Halley couldn't believe what she was hearing. "Our mother, who we haven't seen or heard from since the state took us away as children, came to see you? You've got to be kidding."

Aunt Joy shook her head. "I'm not joking. I wouldn't."

Halley swung her gaze to her silent sister. "You knew," she accused.

"Aunt Joy told me on the way here because I wouldn't stop bugging her about what was wrong."

Phoebe's cheeks were flushed and she was obviously shaken up, too.

"What did she want?" Halley asked.

Aunt Joy fidgeted in her seat. "It's complicated, but I have a feeling you'll both be hearing from her."

Halley slid her hand from her aunt's grasp and wrapped her arms around herself. Her mouth was dry, her heart racing, and her ears buzzed, all signs of an imminent panic attack. She started to take deep, calming breaths.

"Why all of a sudden?" Phoebe spat angrily. "Why now?"

Aunt Joy rose from her seat. "Here's the thing. It's not the first time I've seen her recently." She began pacing back and forth over the large ceramic tiles in the kitchen.

"What does that mean?" Phoebe asked.

"Meg has been out of jail for about six months. She called me when she was released, and I gave her money to help her get on her feet."

Shock rippled through Halley. It didn't seem like her aunt to keep this big of a secret. "Did she ask about us then?" Halley wondered aloud.

"Who cares!" Phoebe yelled at her. "She was a crap mother who let us get taken away, then got herself arrested for possession and intent to sell. She didn't care about us when we were young and needed her. Why do you care now?"

Halley glanced down at her lap. "I don't know why I asked."

But she did. Because a part of her had always wanted to believe there'd been a mistake, that their mother really loved them. That she was sorry for all she'd done.

Wringing her hands, Aunt Joy spoke. "Girls, please. Don't fight with each other. It won't help." She walked over and placed a comforting hand on Halley's shoulder. "And no, honey, she didn't ask about you then. She was scared to start over, and I thought if I gave her money and she'd changed, she'd come back to see you both once she got settled."

"Is that what her visit was about? She's established herself and her life and she's ready to see us?" Halley asked, hating that she still held on to hope where her mother was concerned.

"No." Her aunt's grip on her shoulder tightened. "She ran out of money and wanted more. I asked if she'd gotten a job. If she was self-sufficient or partly so. If she was trying, I would have helped her again. But she wasn't. She isn't. She thinks she's entitled to family money."

"She isn't, though, right? Your parents wrote her out of the will?" she asked of their grandparents, who had passed away before they came to live with their aunt and who had turned their backs on her mother when she ran off to marry a man with no prospects other than serving his country.

"They wrote her out of the will," Aunt Joy said with a nod.

Halley didn't understand her grandparents. All she knew was that Aunt Joy said they were strict, rigid, and their way was the only way. When Meg didn't do what they thought was right for her, they'd shut her out. They hadn't even softened after Halley's father was killed in action.

And when the state stepped in to take them away, only Aunt Joy's father was alive, and he claimed himself incapable of caring for little children. Never mind the fact that he could have afforded full-time help. Joy's father hadn't even told her that her sister had children, never mind that the state had taken them away.

Halley glanced at her sister. Phoebe ran a hand through her hair, pulling on the long strands in fear and frustration.

"And though I would help Meg again if she needed it, I won't enable her," Aunt Joy spoke again after a long silence. "So I think she's going to try and reach out to you two. For money."

"I don't want to see her," Phoebe said.

Halley remained silent. She had mixed feelings. She

couldn't help it. A part of her, the hurt little girl who still lived inside her, was curious about her mom.

"Halley?" Phoebe pushed her for an answer. She wanted to know what Halley planned to do if she heard from her.

"I... I don't know," she admitted.

"Halley!" Phoebe said, appalled.

"Girls, I can't tell you what to do," their aunt chimed in. "You're adults. But I wouldn't be doing right by you if I wasn't honest now. And I'm afraid she's going to play on your emotions to get what she wants, and in the end, you're only going to be hurt."

Halley placed her hand on her aunt's for a quick second, indicating she understood. "I need to think."

"I don't," Phoebe muttered. She rose, leaving her soda unopened on the table. "I need to go. I have phone calls to return for work."

Her sister was angry. Shit. "Phoebe—"

"Not now. We both need to digest all this. Aunt Joy? Will you take me home now?"

Their aunt shot Halley a regret-filled glance. "I'll call you later," she said.

"I'm fine." That was a lie. But she didn't want Aunt Joy worrying even more.

"How will she find us?" Halley couldn't help but ask. "She doesn't know where I live or that you changed our names back to Ward, right?" When they'd returned from foster care, Aunt Joy wanted them to have a fresh start.

Their father had died years ago. His parents were elderly and hadn't taken the girls after foster care stepped in. They, too, had claimed they didn't feel capable of caring for young kids. Juliette was already gone by then, anyway. Again, their aunt had filled in all the blanks. She'd wanted the girls to have the option of changing their last name.

At the time, Phoebe, especially, had clung to their aunt. Halley had done whatever her sister wanted. They'd given up their father's name and taken the family last name.

"I didn't give her your numbers. She knows Phoebe lives in the guesthouse but she doesn't know where, exactly, you live," she said to Halley. "But after Meg left, I realized she played me. She asked if I'd get her water, and when I went to the kitchen, I left my cell phone on the table in the living room. I didn't even think about it until she was gone, but my phone had been moved and she'd been pumping me for information once I refused to write her a check."

Phoebe now folded her arms across her chest. "But cell phones need passwords."

"Umm, I didn't opt to put one on there." Their aunt's cheeks flushed red. "All she had to do was type in your first names. I'm sorry."

"Great," Phoebe muttered.

With a sigh, Aunt Joy turned and started to walk out of the room. She turned. "I'll call you," she said to Halley.

Halley nodded.

After they left, Halley let herself out onto the half-finished deck. Kane wasn't out back. Maybe he'd left without saying good-bye, not wanting to interrupt her. She decided a walk to the ocean was in order. She walked down the stairs on the deck and strolled to the beach. She sat down on the sand, watching the waves lap against the shore in a rhythmic pattern she'd always found soothing.

In her heart and soul, she knew if her mother surfaced, it wouldn't be to have a warm reconciliation or to beg forgiveness. She just wished she didn't find it so hard to accept. As a little girl, she didn't understand why she'd been sent to a new home with people she didn't know. Or why she was so often hungry or bullied by girls as she got older. She'd cry because she missed her mom, or at least, as time went by, wished her mom would come rescue her.

By the time her aunt had shown up, Halley's walls were high. Her anger had come out in spurts, at her aunt for not finding them sooner, at herself for never fitting in. It was always easier to be more introverted, to be alone, than to trust the people around her.

And though she tried more now, as an adult, to be kinder and more forgiving, she was still tied up in knots over the past. It kept her from moving on in any meaningful way. It prevented her from easily giving in to her interest in anything beyond her small, comfortable world.

It kept her from reaching out to Kane.

Chapter Four

KANE HAD GONE to his car to pick up his sander when Halley's visitors walked to their car. He recognized her sister, both from the bar and from times when she'd come to his garage to have her car serviced. He didn't immediately know who the older woman was, but he assumed it was Halley's aunt. She looked enough like Phoebe for him to take an educated guess. They both appeared lost in their own thoughts, frowns on their faces.

He returned to the deck in time to see Halley walking down to the beach, her dress swaying against her legs as she moved. She paused at the water's edge, looking out onto the horizon. Finally, she sat down on the sand, her feet in the water when it made its way up to shore. Even from behind, he could sense the sadness and turmoil rolling off her hunched shoulders.

He wanted to head down there and comfort her. To ask what had happened and how he could make it better. But he knew they weren't at the point where she'd confide in him. If he had his way, they would get there. But for now he'd leave her in peace, as hard as it was for him to do nothing when she was clearly upset.

He got back to work, hard hat and safety goggles on. Halley passed by on her way back inside, treating him to a wave. He smiled back but kept up with the job. A short time later, he glanced up to find her waiting to talk to him.

He turned off the sander, removed his glasses then hat, and met her gaze.

"I thought you might be hungry, so I cooked breakfast. It's a little later than planned because I had visitors, but they're gone and there's food on the table. If you want some."

"You didn't need to cook for me." He rose to his feet. "But I'm glad you did. I just need to wash up first."

She smiled. "Come on in." They walked inside and she directed him to the bathroom.

A few minutes later, he joined her in the kitchen. What appeared to be egg muffins sat on a plate in the center of the table along with delicious-looking bacon strips and a carafe of orange juice.

"This is amazing. And smells delicious." He picked up a napkin and placed it on his lap. "I really appreciate you cooking for me." He took it as a good sign that she wanted him in her house, even if she was just showing her gratitude.

"It was my pleasure. I like cooking. So go ahead. Dig in." She waved her hand toward the food in the middle.

He served her and then himself. Then he took a bite. Damn, she was a good cook. "Fantastic," he said of the muffin. Bacon was bacon. Always good.

"Thank you."

They ate in silence.

"I was named after Halley's Comet," she said, taking him by surprise.

"Really?"

"All of us were named after something in the solar system. You see, before my mother went off the rails with drugs and alcohol, she was smart. A science freak. She loved the planets and outer space, so she named my sisters and me that way. I'm obvious—Halley's Comet. Phoebe is for the outermost moon of Saturn and Juliette for the moon of Uranus. Or so my aunt tells me. I was too young to remember any stories my mother might have told me."

He barely overcame his shock of her opening up to process the wistfulness in her voice at the mention of a sister he'd never heard of. "Sisters? Juliette?" he asked.

She laid down her fork. Sad eyes met his. "I have

two sisters. We have different fathers. I told you about mine and Phoebe's, who died in combat. Well, right before Phoebe and I were sent to foster care, my mother gave Juliette, who had been two at the time, to her father. For cash."

He wasn't sure he'd heard her right. He couldn't have. "Your mother—"

"Sold her daughter. You heard correctly." She pushed herself up from her seat, grabbed her plate, and strode over to the sink. After putting the dish down, she braced a hand on the counter and dipped her head.

Never in his wildest imagination did he think she'd open up this way. But then, she obviously had no one to confide in other than him. He was grateful. He'd take it and listen, even if his heart hurt for her. He couldn't imagine a parent that didn't take care of their children. Even his father, for all his faults, did his best for his kids after Kane's mother passed.

Sensing she needed him, he walked up behind Halley and touched her shoulder, turning her around to face him. "I'm sorry for what you went through. And it sucks that your mother would go to such awful lengths."

Her bottom lip trembled and he had the desire to touch the soft flesh. With his fingers. With his mouth. Anything to comfort her.

"It helps," she murmured. "My mother is back. That's what my aunt wanted when she came by earlier. To tell me that my mother came by for money when she got out of jail." She blew out a long breath, the story obviously draining her.

"You're kidding," he muttered.

Halley shook her head. Then she went back in time and explained more details about her past, including how old she was when the state took her away because her mother was unfit. Just three fucking years old. His hands curled into fists, disgust and pain filling him on her behalf.

"And in the decade that passed, apparently my mother hooked up with a drug dealer," she continued. "So when the police raided the apartment and she was home, they busted her for possession and intent to sell."

He winced. "Jesus."

She sniffed. "And I'm not finished. She sobered up while incarcerated and called my aunt. She told her she had kids, two who were in foster care, and my aunt claimed us. My mother got out six months ago and came to my aunt for money."

"Not to see her girls?" he asked, shocked by the story that was her life.

"No. But my aunt hoped my mother would get her act together and come back to see us." She had settled a hip against the counter. Now she straightened. "My mother came back, all right. And wants more money. Aunt Joy said no and my mother snuck our cell phone numbers from her phone. So I expect to hear from my mother. In fact, I had one hang-up this morning and another one while I was cooking, both from blocked numbers. Phoebe is furious. She wants nothing to do with her."

"And you?"

He grabbed her hand as she spoke. Her sister was mad and her aunt was probably at a loss over what to do.

But Halley? "What do *you* want?" he asked. Because that's what mattered to him. What Halley wanted or needed.

No one had given her that before. No one had been there for her as a child and it was obvious she didn't let anyone in now. He wanted to be her person.

"I want... to go back and erase the past. Barring that, which I know is impossible, I want my mother to come forward now and have changed. To be the person I missed all those years in foster care," she admitted, her voice trembling. "Does that mean I need to meet her and see for myself? Do I need to be hit upside the head with a two-by-four, or can I take my aunt's word for the fact that she's selfish and only wants money?" She sighed. "When I say it out loud, I know the answer," she said before he could comment. "I just wish…"

"I know," he said, squeezing her hand. "I understand dealing with a parent with an addiction. My dad has a thing for gambling. I'm usually the one who steps up to be the adult."

She shook her head and let out a soft laugh. "That's a pretty crappy thing for us to have in common."

He chuckled. "Well, it's something. But I do think you should follow your heart and not what your sister or aunt thinks is right."

"Thank you," she murmured.

"For what?"

"For listening. For not judging."

"I'm happy to be there for you. Any time."

"I guess you earned another home-cooked meal," she said, smiling brighter now.

"You've got yourself a deal. I'll try to come by after work this week depending on how busy we get at the garage."

He grasped her shoulders and leaned in close, inhaling a hint of a fruity scent in her hair. One that went straight to his dick and made him hard. He wanted to kiss her pretty pink lips, to slide his tongue inside her sweet mouth, but after she'd unloaded all her pain, to act on his desire would be taking advantage of her. And that he wouldn't do.

There would be another time. He was sure of it.

✧   ✧   ✧

THE WEEK HAD been a hectic one at the garage, and by the time Friday rolled around, Kane was exhausted. Although he'd have liked to make it over to Halley's one or two of those evenings, they were overloaded with repairs and he'd been working late. He needed to hire another mechanic and he'd have to get on that soon.

And though the part for her SUV had arrived, he'd been out on a service call when she'd come in to pay and pick up the vehicle. He was left wondering how she was doing, if she'd heard from her mother, and whether or not she'd thought about him at all. Yeah, he had it bad. Something he wasn't used to at all.

He'd gone out for an hour last night but he hadn't run into Halley at the Blue Wall and he wasn't surprised. She'd been dragged there by her sister last week. Maybe he could convince her to join him one night... and actually enjoy herself.

Early Saturday morning, his phone woke him, startling him out of sleep. He rolled over and grabbed his cell.

"Hello?" he asked, without checking who was calling first.

"Hi, Kane." He recognized his sister's voice.

He rubbed his eyes with the back of his hand. "Why are you waking me at the crack of dawn?" he asked with a yawn.

"Is Dad with you?"

"What?" That woke Kane up fast and he sat upright in bed. "Why would he be here when he lives with you?" he asked, a sinking feeling in his gut.

He looked around his room and saw his jeans on the floor. "Didn't he babysit last night?" He always watched Nicky when Andrea worked her shift at the Blue Wall.

"No. He said he wanted to go out with Walter and Pete," she said, naming their father's oldest friends. One of whom liked a good card game as much as Joe.

He tucked the phone in his ear and climbed out of bed, reaching for his pants. "You think he pulled an all-nighter?" Whenever their dad would go to a high-stakes poker game and drag himself home late, their mother would say he'd pulled an all-nighter.

"I don't know but he hasn't checked in and I'm worried."

He pulled on his jeans and grabbed a shirt from a drawer. "Don't worry. I'll go to his usual haunts. Donny has a place above his pub. He runs games out of there."

"Thanks, Kane."

"Don't thank me. It's what I do. I'll call you when I find him." He disconnected the call.

He finished getting ready, ran downstairs, wishing he had time for coffee, grabbed his keys, and headed out. He stopped first at Walter's, hoping the old man was home with his wife, but no luck. Edna said he hadn't come home last night, but unlike his father, he'd called. Told her he was feeling lucky because his palms were itchy, an old superstition that meant he was coming into money. Edna was used to her husband doing his own thing and didn't think anything of it. The only issue was Walter hadn't said where he was going.

Which was fine. Kane could guess.

He arrived at Donny's Pub and headed around back, walking up the stairs to the back room. He banged on the door hard, and when no one answered, he banged again.

"Hold your horses," a voice inside yelled.

Kane leaned against the doorframe. The door swung open wide and Donny, eyes bloodshot, met his gaze. Donny, who had inherited the bar from his father but wasn't as smart, gripped the door. His salt-and-pepper hair stood on end. "Joey's boy," he said.

Kane pushed the door open, causing Donny to stumble back. "Where's my father?"

"Easy." He held up both hands. "Joe, your kid's

here." He looked at Kane. "Back there."

He gestured to the living room, where his father was passed out on one side of a beat-up old sofa with holes in the fabric. Walter was on an old piece-of-shit chair and ottoman, also out cold.

"Dad." Kane slapped his father's cheek. "Dad. Wake up."

Walter could wake up and head home on his own time.

"What the—" Joe shook his head and pushed himself to a sitting position on the sofa. "How'd you find me?"

"Where else would you be, Dad?" Kane asked wearily, despite the fact that he'd barely just woken up himself.

"I had a good night," he said, patting his full pockets, as if winning excused him from falling back into old, bad habits.

"Did Walter?"

His father laughed, the sound dry and rusty. "Lost his shirt."

Kane shook his head. "So much for superstition," he muttered.

"Get yourself together and let's go." He assumed Walter had driven and could get himself home.

He walked out in silence and got into the car, waiting for his father to climb into the passenger seat of his Camaro. Finally, they headed home. Kane drummed the fingers of one hand on the wheel. His anger had been building since his sister called and told him his father was missing. It had only grown, his father's glib pronouncement of having a good night feeding his exasperation.

"Did you even think to call Andrea? She was worried when she realized you didn't come home last night." He glanced to the side.

His father's eye twitched. "I meant to but the game started and I got sidetracked."

Kane blew out a sharp breath. "Yeah? Well, it's damned selfish if you ask me. And didn't you promise to cut out the gambling?"

He'd never been able to get his father into any kind of addiction treatment program. Even at his lowest, when he'd lost his wife and was in such serious debt that he'd had to take a second mortgage on the house, he'd refused to go.

With a groan, his father shifted in his seat, facing him. "I should have called. I'll apologize. But I won. She'll be happy."

"Trust me, she won't be," Kane muttered. He gripped the wheel tight in his hand. "Dad, you cannot run off and piss away money. You won't always win. You *know* this." He reined in his frustration, because when it came to his father and this subject, *he* never won.

After dropping his dad off at home, Kane headed over to Halley's. Jackson had assured him he had things under control at the garage, so he had the day to himself.

A day to handle his side job and catch up with Halley. After his shitty morning, he needed something to offset the frustration his father caused, and being around Halley helped to soften him inside and make him feel better.

✧   ✧   ✧

THE SUN SHONE over the ocean, reflecting off the water, as Halley looked out the window from her seat in front of the easel. Her work was always dark, intense, suiting the mood she usually found herself in, but again today, streaks of lighter colors found their way onto the canvas. She didn't know what to make of the change but she didn't fight the muse.

Lost in work, she was startled when the sound of a drill cut into her concentration.

"Kane," she murmured, her stomach fluttering with sudden awareness. Putting down her brush, she rose and walked into the kitchen. As she washed up, cleaning the paint off her hands and arms, she thought back to when she'd seen him last week.

Since then, she kept returning to their conversation. She was shocked at how much she'd revealed to Kane. She never confided in anyone, let alone about her family history, but he'd been there right after an upsetting conversation with her aunt and sister, he'd wanted to listen, and God, had she needed an ear. An objective point of view about a subject she could never be detached about.

He'd asked her what she wanted and hadn't told her what to do, unlike her sister, who had, again on the phone, been adamant about neither of them speaking to or seeing their mother if she surfaced. Phoebe might not be happy that Halley was entertaining the notion, but if she acted on her desire to see her mother again? Phoebe would be furious. Undecided still, Halley forced her mind off the unpleasant subject and on to one much easier to take.

Kane. She might find him ridiculously attractive and want him sexually, but there was something about him that had always gotten to her on a deeper level. Because he had a good soul and an even better heart. He'd reached out to her when she was obviously in need and had been there for her when they barely knew one another. Now? He was slowly ingratiating himself into her life. And she was having trouble finding the will to care.

So despite telling herself she was being silly, she went into the bedroom, looked in the mirror, fixed her hair, and swiped a quick hint of gloss on her lips.

She hoped he'd knock or let her know he was there, but he didn't, and after an hour, she decided to go out and see if he needed anything. But first she went back to the kitchen and poured a glass of ice water, then headed out to the deck.

Not wanting to interrupt him, she waited for him to notice her. Besides, watching him work was no hardship. The pull and flex of his muscles was a treat and she ogled him without shame, until finally, he glanced up.

She held up the glass for him to see.

"One sec." He shut off the machine he was using and pulled off his hard hat and goggles. He walked over, taking the drink from her. "Thank you. I could use it."

He gulped down the contents of the glass in what felt like four big swallows and wiped the sweat from his forehead with the back of his arm. "Damn, it's hot out today."

She took in the moisture dampening his shirt. "Want to come in for a little while? The air conditioning will feel good."

He shook his head. "I'm going to keep working."

She glanced at his serious expression and furrowed brows. He wasn't his usual smiling self. "Is anything wrong?" she asked.

He met her gaze. "Shitty morning."

She felt for him and knew what it was like to have problems you didn't know how to solve. "I'm a good listener." The offer was the least she could do after she'd confided in him the last time they were together.

He shook his head and grunted his reply. "Nothing you want to hear."

"Really? Because I remember dumping on you the other day and you seemed to want to listen. Why wouldn't I do the same?" she asked, not taking his dismissal as definitive.

His lips lifted a little at the reminder. "Okay, then. I'll take you up on that."

Everything inside her eased. "Good. Now, I always find it better to brood down by the water. Want to take a break and talk there?" she asked.

He shrugged, his muscles moving beneath his shirt. "Why not? Maybe it'll help."

She placed the glass down by the sliding door and kicked off her shoes.

He glanced at her bare feet and shook his head. "I'm working with nails. I'd rather not have to rush you to the hospital."

"Gotcha." The last thing she wanted was to get hurt and need a tetanus shot. Ugh. She slid her sandals back on and led the way down the stairs and across the sandy expanse leading to the water.

They sat down in what she liked to think of as *her spot* and kicked off her sandals once more, sliding her feet forward so when the water lapped up the shore, it covered her toes before receding again. He didn't remove his shoes but settled in beside her, keeping his work boots safe from the water.

"How's the painting going?" he asked.

"Good. Something feels a little different but I'm going with it."

He nodded. "Follow your muse."

"That's the plan. Maybe different is good. I mean, every summer I hope that one of the big New York gallery owners ends up seeing my work and asking me to show in Manhattan. They haven't so far but I keep hoping anyway." Because summers brought the wealthy vacationers and winter just brought snow, she thought to herself.

He shaded his eyes with a hand and glanced at her. "You could beat the pavement," he said. "Go to the city and show them your paintings yourself."

"Have you met me?" she asked, laughing. "Did I ever give you the impression I'm the type of person to head to the city and push my work on unsuspecting gallery owners?"

He tilted his head, amusement lighting his handsome features. "You could try and step outside your comfort zone."

She merely laughed harder. No one was more a creature of habit and home comforts than her. "You sound like Phoebe."

"Because we both want what's best for you."

She leaned back against her hands. "And who would know that better than me?" she asked.

He looked out over the ocean and let out a low groan. He wasn't thinking about her art, that much she knew. But she also understood that someone would only speak when and if they were ready. So she waited, focusing on the scenery, because otherwise she would look to her right again and drink him in. His strong profile, straight nose, full lips. Not that she'd noticed and memorized his profile or anything.

"My sister called this morning," he said at last. "My dad didn't come home last night. I found him at an all-night poker game with his friends."

She winced. "Ouch. I'm sorry."

"Thing is, he knows better. And he fucking won, which means he's going to think he's invincible and keep going, looking for bigger and better games until he loses and gets in serious debt." He kicked at the sand with his big boot.

She sighed. "Addiction is hard and not just on the addict."

He nodded in agreement. "It's been going on for years. When we were growing up, one year, my mother had been saving for Christmas. I don't remember how old I was. Maybe twelve or so. And Dad, he had this bright idea that he could double her small savings and get me and Andi even better gifts."

She held her breath, knowing where the story was going and almost afraid to hear.

"He lost it all. Dragged himself home and had to face my mother's wrath. Andi and I heard the yelling from our rooms." He swallowed hard. "Mom sold her sewing machine that year to make sure we didn't miss Christmas. And the thing is, what Dad didn't understand was that we didn't want big presents. We just wanted a fucking holiday. A few gifts under the tree like the other kids so when we went to school and people asked what we got, we didn't have to say nothing."

"And your mother gave that to you. She sounds like a special person." She was probably where Kane had gotten his warmth and generous spirit.

"She really was." His expression softened. "There was nothing she wouldn't do for her family. And we lost her too soon. Her death threw Dad into a spiral he's still digging his way out of with a second mortgage on his house."

She surprised herself by reaching out and placing her hand over his. "You can only do so much to help him. Obviously, you can't change his habits, and he clearly isn't interested in stopping. But you can alter your reaction to him. You need to divest yourself of the need to fix him or you're going to drive yourself insane."

He snorted at that. "Easier said than done. But you're smart and you're right. I need to work on it." He turned toward her and she shifted her weight so she was closer to him.

"Did it help to talk?" she asked, knowing it had lifted a burden off of her when he'd listened.

"It all helped. Talking, the water… you." He stared into her eyes, the dark brown depths sparkling with something that beckoned to her.

Seconds passed. The roar of the ocean waves mixed with the swell of noise echoing in her ears as he leaned toward her. His lips called to hers. She didn't know who moved first but suddenly they connected. Meshed. Harmonized in utter perfection. He glided his mouth over hers, back and forth until she parted her lips, letting him in.

The warmth of the sun beat down at the same time heat filled her from the sensuality of the kiss. He brought a hand up to cup her neck, his hard grip an erotic counterpoint to the softness of his mouth. He sucked on her bottom lip and nipped with his teeth, causing her to moan and lean in, needing to get closer to him.

Over and over, his lips slid over hers, alternately sipping, then devouring, his tongue thrusting into the deep recesses of her mouth, the thrust and parry of his tongue a prelude of how he'd take her body. Gentle sometimes, rougher others, both ways erotic and hot, arousing her mind as well as her body.

He gripped her neck tighter and pulled her to him, her breasts crushing against the cotton of his shirt. Her nipples were hard and needy and she wished she could rub them against his hair-roughened chest. Instead she was stuck with a kiss and soft whimpers escaping her throat.

He nipped at her lip one last time, swiped his tongue over her in a soothing motion before pulling back and gazing into her eyes.

"So much better than I fucking imagined," he said in a gruff voice.

She let out a hesitant laugh as reality drifted back and settled on her shoulders. "Kane…"

"No regrets," he warned her.

She shook her head. "I don't. I can't regret that kiss. But you need to know, I'm not a good bet for a relationship."

He narrowed his gaze, that heady stare still hot on hers. "What makes you say that?"

She swallowed hard. "I'm different. You know that about me. I like being alone. I work hard, get lost in my paintings. I forget what time it is. Sometimes I don't pay attention to days and nights. I spend more time alone than with people and most guys don't want a girl they can't take out with their friends because she doesn't like big crowds." There. She'd said it all, put her truths out there for him to hear.

Not all of her truths, of course. There were some she didn't drag into the light of day. Ever. She didn't even allow them in her nightmares if she could help it. The problem was, sometimes she couldn't control her dreams. She wished she could.

"And?" he asked, as if what she'd said meant nothing.

"I've had unsuccessful relationships. And do you want to know why they were unsuccessful? Because I'm odd," she said before he could answer. "And they got frustrated with me and broke things off. So I don't do relationships anymore. I don't like disappointing people and I don't like being hurt when things inevitably end."

"Hmm."

She opened her eyes wide. "That's all you have to say? Hmm?"

An understanding smile curved his lips. "You're forgetting that I know you and I like what I see. I'm not looking to change you. And I'm not looking to force you into a relationship you don't want."

She blinked and braced herself up with a hand on the sand. "You aren't?"

He shook his head. "I like *you*. I like spending time with you. And yeah, I like kissing you. A fuck of a lot. And I plan to do it more often. But trap you in a relationship if that's not what you want?" He shook his head. "Not happening."

She swiped her tongue over her kiss-roughened lips. "I don't know what to say." Nor did she know what to make of his proclamation and easy acceptance.

"I like you and you like me, yes?"

She nodded.

"And the kiss, it was good?" he asked, stroking a hand down her cheek and eliciting a shiver that went straight to her already erect and aware nipples and down to her sex.

"Yes," she murmured.

"Then let's not overanalyze or examine what this is or isn't. My life is crazy what with the garage, my father, my nephew who hangs around every day... and now a side gig that I definitely enjoy." He gestured back to her deck. "No need to label and complicate things."

She was surprised to hear him be so nonchalant. With his pursuit of a date and him showing up here to build her deck in his limited spare time, she definitely thought he wanted something serious.

If he didn't, if he could accept who she was and what she could give, then she didn't see an issue with letting things be and taking it one day at a time.

"So are we on the same page?" he asked, his lips brushing over hers. "We have fun? We enjoy each other? And we don't put pressure on either one of us with expectations?"

"Agreed," she said, wondering why her stomach tumbled over the idea that he didn't want her for anything more than just a good time. He'd given her exactly what she'd asked for.

They sat for a while longer, looking out at the ocean. She loved the feel of sand between her toes and water lapping over her feet. It soothed her like nothing else in her life ever had. And having this man by her side? Utter perfection.

Suddenly a big black dog came barreling toward them, flying into them and coming up from his head butt of her stomach licking everything in sight.

She laughed and grabbed his collar. "Bruno, you bad boy. Did you escape your house again?" She giggled into his soft fur.

"Hey, boy." Kane patted his furry head. "Are you an escapee?" he asked.

The dog licked his cheek.

Kane grinned, earning himself points in Halley's book. Any man who liked dogs rose in her estimation.

And Bruno was discriminating. She'd seen him growl at the neighbor on the other side of Halley's house who hated dogs and complained when Bruno escaped his home, which admittedly was too often.

Kane picked up a stick within reaching distance of where they sat. "Do you fetch?" he asked the dog, tossing the stick.

Bruno took off, running for the new toy and delivering it back to Kane, dropping it at his feet. "Good boy," he said, running his hand over the dog's fur.

For the next few minutes, they played fetch until Ronnie, Halley's neighbor, sauntered over to retrieve her dog. "Sorry for the interruption," she said, taking in first Halley, then Kane, her eyes lighting up when she looked at him.

Blonde, single, pretty, and obviously interested in Kane, she waited around instead of grabbing her dog and returning home.

Which meant introductions were in order. "Kane, meet my neighbor Ronnie Palmer. Ronnie, this is my... *friend*, Kane Harmon," she said, struggling over the word choice to describe their relationship while Ronnie's eyes lit up at that revelation.

Halley's stomach tumbled at the sexual recognition the pretty woman gave Kane. "Ronnie is renting the house next door for the month," she murmured.

"Why haven't I seen you around before?" Ronnie

asked, with eyes only for him.

"I own the garage in town. Maybe your car just hasn't broken down?" He shaded his eyes from the sun with a hand, looking up at Halley's neighbor.

She straightened further, pushing out her ample cleavage over her sheer bikini cover-up. "Well, isn't that perfect? I just happen to need an oil change," Ronnie said. "Maybe I'll come by the garage instead of going to the gas station." She fluttered her lashes.

"I'll see you then," Kane said. "And nice to meet you."

Halley swallowed a groan at Ronnie's pleased smile. She'd been adamant about not labeling their relationship, but being Kane's friend with no expectations was going to be harder than she'd imagined.

"Come on, Bruno," Ronnie said and sashayed her way across the beach, her dog following after her.

Kane leaned back on his hands. "So she seems typical of our town's summer visitors."

"What do you mean?" Halley asked.

"Beautiful, forward, and probably only interested in one thing," he said, obviously not interested in what the blonde had to offer.

The twisting discomfort in Halley's stomach eased. "Someone doesn't like the tourists much. Don't they bring in good money over the summers for your garage?" she asked.

He nodded. "They do. But you'd be right in saying I'm not a big fan." He rose to his feet and extended a hand. "I need to get back to work."

She recognized a subject change and placed her palm in his and he helped her stand. Together they walked back to the house, leaving Halley with churning emotions and a lot to think about when it came to her non-relationship with Kane Harmon.

Chapter Five

*H*AVE FUN. ENJOY *each other. No pressure, no expectations.* No, they were not on the same page, Kane thought, but he had a plan and he was sticking to it. He'd given Halley what he knew she needed to hear if he was going to keep seeing her. Talking to her. Kissing her. And fucking her. Eventually.

For now, he'd settle for what she was willing to give while he sweet-talked her into more. He worked into the afternoon, and the few times he paused, wiping the sweat from his brow and looking through the glass, he saw her painting. She was a study in concentration, more so because he was using power tools, which had to be distracting for her. Her brush moved across the canvas with deliberate precision, her eyes focused, never drifting to his.

When he stepped in for a better look, he noticed her little tongue peeking out from between her lips.

Which brought him back to their kiss, one he wouldn't be forgetting any time soon.

Her lips were soft and sensual, the gliding touch of her tongue electrifying. It had taken all his self-control not to lay her down in the sand, strip her out of that sexy dress, and take her right there in front of God, the water, and the fucking neighbor who'd ended up interrupting their time together.

He was ready to wrap up for the day, so he knocked on the glass sliding door to let her know.

She slid it open and stepped out. "What's up?"

He immediately took in her paint-stained hands, a smudge of light blue on her cheek, and bit back a grin. "I'm finished for the day. I need to do some things for my family tomorrow, so I won't be working on the deck."

"You don't need to account to me. It's not like you're on the clock. I'm just grateful you're finishing this for me at all," she murmured.

"Okay then. I wanted to say good-bye," he said.

She grinned. "Good-bye, Kane."

He smiled wide. "So long, beautiful."

He liked the flush that always stained her cheeks when he used that word. He started to turn, then paused. "Have you heard from your mother?" From her carefree demeanor, he doubted it, but he needed to ask.

She bit down on her lower lip. "No… but I have had one hang-up. Maybe she's nervous to talk to me?" she asked almost hopefully.

He was really worried about the situation, though he'd never let on to Halley. He figured her aunt had good reason and knowledge to be concerned about her mother's motives. On the other hand, he understood Halley's need to know the woman, and if she was disappointed in the end, at least she'd take heart knowing she'd tried to give the woman a chance.

Kane just didn't want her heart broken, and he'd be there to pick up the pieces if the worst occurred. "I guess you'll see what happens."

She nodded, her hand on the edge of the slider, as if waiting to close the door behind him.

"One more thing," he said.

"What's that?" She tipped her head to the side curiously.

In for a penny, he thought. "I was hoping you'd do me a favor," he said, pushing his luck and he knew it.

"Name it." She obviously felt she owed him for the deck work, something he was shamelessly trading on… and she'd realize it as soon as he told her what he desired.

"Tomorrow night is a family dinner. On Sundays we get together at Dad and Andi's house. She and Nicky live with him," he added by way of explanation.

"Anyway, it's casual. But I was hoping you'd come with me."

Her eyes opened wide. "Kane…"

He reached out and grasped her paint-speckled hand. "It's not a big deal. I just want you to be my buffer so I don't get into it with Dad and end up upsetting everyone in the process. Please," he said before she could argue.

"But you said yourself it's a family dinner and I'm sure I don't belong there."

He shook his head, anticipating this argument. "Wrong. Dad often has a friend come, sometimes Nicky brings someone from school or camp. Dinner is just an excuse to get us all together. It doesn't matter if someone else joins in." He raised an eyebrow. "So what do you say?"

"I—"

"Pretty please?"

"You're not going to stop until I say yes, are you?"

He lifted one shoulder in a half shrug. "Nope."

Her wavering smile turned true and she laughed. "Fine. I'll go." She sounded nervous and he'd make sure she both showed up and was at ease.

"Thank you. I'll pick you up around five forty-five tomorrow. Dress casual. And don't worry. We're typically normal," he promised. "You'll be fine."

She looked at him uncertainly, like she wasn't sure

she believed him. She would, soon. Because he had an ulterior motive in inviting her, one that involved showing her that she wasn't the only one with a dysfunctional family. Considering there wasn't a family dinner that passed without a mention of his father's bad habits, Kane wanted Halley to see that family was messy.

One of the reasons she withdrew into herself was because she hadn't grown up with family around her. She got upset when her sister was angry, pulled away from her aunt, who tried to win her over with extravagant gifts. And she hid inside her house to avoid it all.

It was all obvious to him.

But if he could show her how normal it was to be around family who loved you despite your faults, he could open her up to new experiences, both with her family and hopefully with him.

It wasn't a purely selfish desire, either.

Of course, he wanted her to be with him willingly, in a relationship she didn't mind acknowledging publicly. But he also wanted to give her family back to her. In a way that didn't make her want to curl up and be alone because she felt odd, in her words, or different.

He raised a hand, knowing it was time to leave before she changed her mind. "Bye, Halley."

She smiled back at him. "Bye, Kane."

✧　✧　✧

ON SUNDAY AFTERNOON, closer to evening, Halley stood in front of a full-length mirror behind her bedroom door, taking in the pile of clothing on the bed behind her. She'd already tried on a few dresses and a pair of jeans. Now she stood in her bra and panties, completely undecided.

What did casual mean? A dress like she wore every day to paint? Or a pair of jeans that she didn't really like wearing in the summer because she hated the feeling of denim sticking to her skin in the heat and humidity but really did meet the definition of casual?

She was about to pull yet another dress from her closet when her cell rang. Her sister's name flashed on the screen.

"Hi, Phoebe."

"What are you doing?" her sister asked. Sometimes Halley thought Phoebe had radar, catching her at the most inopportune times. Like when Kane had been working on her deck.

She bit down on the inside of her cheek. "I'm trying to decide what to wear."

"Since when? Throw on a dress and call it a day. That's what your closet is filled with anyway. Oh. Wait. Why are you getting dressed when the day's about to end? Where are you going so close to dinner time?" her snoopy sibling asked.

She really didn't want to tell her but she could use the advice. "Kane asked me to go to dinner at his father's house," she admitted.

"I knew it! He's into you."

"We're *friends*," she insisted. If friends kissed. Hot, steamy, sensual kisses on the beach like in the movies. "He wants me as a buffer because he has some family issues." Ones she wouldn't tell her sister about because she would keep Kane's secrets to herself.

"Sure you are. Okay, what are you choosing between?"

"One of my dresses or a pair of jeans and a tee shirt. He said be casual."

Phoebe paused, obviously thinking.

"Be yourself. You're a floaty-dress kind of girl. Don't change for any man," her sister advised her.

"I wasn't trying to change. I just didn't want to stand out."

Phoebe cleared her throat. "If this were anyone else, I'd think they were silly, but because it's you, I know this is serious. For one thing, you never go out on a date and this makes it a big deal. And for another, you rarely go out at all, which makes it a bigger deal. Either way, be yourself. Wear one of your pretty dresses. And relax. Nobody there will bite, I'm sure. Or maybe Kane will if you ask him nicely."

"Phoebe!" Halley said, laughing. "Behave yourself."

"What fun would that be? Want me to come over and help you pick something out?"

Halley sighed. "No. I don't have that kind of time."

"Then wear something with blue in it. It matches your eyes."

"Thank you," she murmured.

"Any time. And you owe me a dinner. I was calling to see if Jamie and I could come by for your fantastic cooking."

Halley smiled. If not for her sister's pushy—in a good kind of way—personality, Halley wouldn't see nearly enough of her sister or her nephew. "You've got yourself a deal."

She chose a pastel white-and-light-blue everyday dress, as Phoebe suggested, with a pair of strappy silver sandals. Something she'd wear if she was just going into town for an errand, but one she wouldn't paint in because she liked it too much to risk ruining it.

She put on minimal makeup because that's who she was. She didn't overdo the foundation, eye shadow, or lipstick. She wasn't into the whole made-up look, and Kane seemed to like her as she was. Although she told herself this wasn't a date, she had no doubt it was something. Every tummy flutter and wave of nerves confirmed that.

A little while later, Kane picked her up in his Camaro, wearing a pair of dark denim jeans, cleaner than the ones he wore during the week to work, but which fit his lean frame the same way. With his hunter-green tee shirt, he looked rugged and sexy.

He whistled when he caught sight of her. "Looking beautiful, beautiful."

She blushed. "I baked cookies for dessert. And as a thank you to your family for having me."

"You didn't need to but I'm glad you did. What kind?" he asked, eyes twinkling.

"Chocolate chip."

"A girl after my own heart. You ready?" he asked.

She grabbed her purse and the cookies covered in tinfoil. He held the dish so she could lock up the house, and they headed to his car.

A little while later, they pulled up in front of a well-maintained house with manicured shrubbery on a residential street. With light gray clapboard and black shutters and a white front door, it looked warm and welcoming.

Nicky was shooting baskets into a hoop at the far end of the driveway when they pulled in.

Kane climbed out of the car and walked around to her side. "Hey, sport. How's it going?" he called to his nephew.

"Good! Want to play?" Nicky asked, dribbling the

ball and shooting it toward the basket, missing by an inch.

"I promise to shoot a few before I leave. Right now, let me introduce Halley to your mom, okay?"

"Okay." The boy turned back to his practicing.

"He's adorable."

"And a good kid," Kane said. "I'm glad my sister doesn't have a pain in the ass like me to deal with."

Halley frowned. "From all you've told me, I think you were just as good as Nicky."

"Maybe until puberty hit," he muttered.

She grinned and they headed up the walk. He let them into the house, where a set of stairs was immediately in front of them. They walked up and she found them facing the kitchen. To the right was a living room and around to the left of that was a dining room.

"Kane!" A pretty woman with dark brown hair pulled into a ponytail walked out of the kitchen to meet them. "And you must be Halley. Welcome."

"Nice to meet you," Halley said. "And thank you for having me."

"Any time. Ooh, what is that? It smells delicious!" Andi said.

Halley handed her the plate of cookies. "Chocolate chip."

Andi accepted the plate. "Thank you! Come on inside. Dinner's almost ready. Dad's grilling steak. I hope you eat red meat?" She turned to Halley. "I can throw chicken on the grill if you prefer."

"Steak is fine. Don't worry. Can I do anything to help?"

"Nope. Why don't you call Nicky in, Kane," Andi said. "And then we'll sit down."

Not long after, they were all seated at the table. Halley was, as Kane promised, comfortable with his family. His father was charming, despite his flaws, and he talked to Halley about her painting when Kane mentioned it. Andi, who was obviously a doting mom and doing a great job as a single parent, was also sweet and warm.

She found herself relaxing when, midway through the meal, Nicky said, "Uncle Kane, want to play cards with me?"

"What game?" Kane asked.

"Poker."

Andi coughed and dropped her fork onto the table. "You don't know how to play poker."

"Grandpa taught me! We can play with Cheerios until I have real money," he said. "Then, when I'm older, Grandpa's gonna teach me how to really gamble."

Kane's gaze zeroed in on his father, and Halley stiffened for the fallout.

"Nicky, please go outside and play until dessert,"

Andi said to the boy, who'd already finished eating and had been fidgeting in his seat anyway. Her hands were curling into fists on the table.

As if sensing his mom's upset, he scrambled out of his seat and ran to go outside.

Andi waited until Nicky was out of earshot before turning to her father. "You taught my son how to play poker and to gamble?" she asked angrily.

"It's just a card game, darlin'."

"Don't darlin' me. The games are harmless but gambling sure as hell isn't. You're an addict, Dad. And addiction runs in the family. I don't need you exposing my son to gambling with Cheerios or money. It's careless and stupid."

"The boy needs to know these things. It's a life skill," he argued.

Andi thumped her hand on the table and rose to her feet.

Kane caught her hand in his and urged her to sit back down with softly murmured words.

Then he turned to his father. "Dad, Andi is raising her son her way. You know how we both feel about gambling. That means you need to respect her wishes. Don't teach Nicky bad habits and don't go behind her back. Because if you'd given it any thought, you'd know she wouldn't like it." He kept his tone measured, but Halley sensed the leashed anger inside him.

Halley felt like an observer to a movie except this was real life, and she felt guilty for being here when something so serious was happening.

"Maybe I should—"

Kane stopped her next words with a well-placed hand on her thigh. "It's fine," he said to her. "Stay put."

She swallowed hard.

"Fine," his father finally said, in a child-like sulking voice. "I won't play with my grandkid," he said, deliberately misunderstanding her point.

Andi groaned and put her head in her hands. Then she rose and began clearing the table.

In the silence that remained, Joe Harmon also stood. "Excuse me. I have things to do," he muttered and walked out.

"I think that's the end of the meal," Kane said, turning toward Halley and shooting her a sad glance.

"Let me help your sister." She pushed her chair back and began collecting plates. Kane helped, and while Andi cleaned, she and Kane cleared the table.

Andi insisted she could handle the rest on her own and all but begged them to go do whatever they wanted. "Let's go outside," he suggested.

She followed him out the front door. Then, while he and his nephew played a friendly game of H-O-R-S-E, she watched the two males dribble and shoot and have fun. It was nice seeing Kane interact with the young boy, teaching him pointers on the game and things that would help him when his league started again in the winter. Not to mention, he didn't suggest they leave until he'd fulfilled his promise to the boy to play hoops with him, something she admired.

Once he'd exhausted the child, he sent him inside. They stopped in to say good-bye to Andi. His father was hidden away somewhere and they left him alone.

Back in the car, he turned on the ignition, set the air conditioning, and met her gaze. "I gotta say, my plan to take you to a normal family dinner backfired. This was way worse than usual."

She smiled and placed a hand on his forearm, feeling the strength in his muscles there. "It's fine. I enjoyed your family. I'm just sorry if I made things more uncomfortable by being there."

"You didn't. Dad did that all on his own. What was he thinking teaching a seven-year-old the basics of gambling when he knows it's an issue for himself?"

She shrugged. "He doesn't seem to want to acknowledge that at all."

"True." He placed a hand on the wheel. "Sorry we missed out on your cookies." He pouted at the realization.

"It's fine. I hope Nicky enjoys them. And I can always make it up to you with a fresh batch."

He grinned. "That makes me a happy man. Now… what do you say to some Italian ices? Ever been to Hank's?"

She shook her head. "I've passed it but there's always been a ridiculous crowd of people out front."

"Well, it's worth the wait. Feel like going on the way home?"

She nodded. "If you can keep me occupied while we wait, then I don't mind."

He laughed. "I think I like that challenge."

When they arrived at Hank's, an outdoor ice cream and Italian ices stand, they discovered a short line. Not enough for him to have to entertain her, and before they knew it, they were ordering.

Because they also had ice cream, Halley changed her mind when it came to ordering and asked for vanilla ice cream with hot fudge topping. Kane got a red Italian ice.

They took their desserts and walked over to a short brick wall and hopped up, sitting side by side, legs swinging as they ate.

He finished his first. "Good?" he asked, putting his cup down beside him.

She glanced over, laughing. "Your tongue is red."

He stuck it out at her and grinned.

"Want some of mine?" She held out the spoon of vanilla and chocolate mixed.

"No, doesn't exactly mix with my cherry." He paused, as if thinking of something. "Unless..."

"Hmm?" She raised an eyebrow.

"Unless I'm kissing you." And before she could react, he leaned over and swept his tongue over her lips and into her mouth, devouring her quickly but thoroughly.

She moaned into him, leaning in close, savoring the warm cherry flavor he brought to her dessert.

Before she was ready, he lifted his head and met her gaze, his eyes dark and hungry. "Now that is how to eat an ice cream."

Her perky nipples and needy sex agreed.

✧   ✧   ✧

KANE PARKED IN front of Halley's house and braced his hand on the steering wheel, unwilling to leave her just yet. That kiss had lit a fire in him that needed quenching, and a good-bye peck wasn't going to do it. Until tonight, he wouldn't have said she seemed ready for that next step, but she appeared more relaxed around him now and she definitely wanted him as much as he desired her. One thing he knew, he wasn't letting her go without at least an attempt at taking things further.

Before she could let herself out, he hit the button on the automatic locks, closing her in.

"What are you doing?" she asked.

"Before I get out of the car, there's something you need to know."

Curious eyes met his. "What is it?" she asked.

"If I walk you to your front door, I'm not leaving." His words lay hot and heavy between them, leaving no doubt as to his intention and desires.

He waited for understanding to dawn, and when it did, her eyes darkened to a deeper hue. "Kane," she said, more breathlessly than before.

"What's it going to be, beautiful?"

She swiped her tongue over her bottom lip. His dick perked up at the sensual gesture.

"Get out of the car." Her voice was deep and husky, a definite current of sexual desire flowing from her words.

Relief flowed through him that they were on the same page. He shut the engine, telling himself to calm the fuck down so he didn't jump her the minute they got through the door. Just because she'd agreed didn't mean she was ready for a fast, hard tumble. A woman like Halley deserved more.

He wanted to give her more.

He came around her side of the car and placed a hand on the small of her back, leading her up the path and to the house. She pulled her key from her purse and put it in the lock with shaky hands. He grasped the key and inserted it into the lock for her. He was steadier but not by much.

Once inside, away from passing cars and prying eyes, he grabbed her purse, tossed it onto the nearest chair, and pulled her into him.

She gasped at the needy way he banded her against him, holding her close with his arms, his head coming down, his mouth capturing hers. Their tongues tangled, dueled, their hands fumbling with clothing.

She grabbed the hem of his shirt and pulled it over his head. He pushed the elastic neckline of her dress down, revealing her breasts to him, as they overflowed the cups of her lacy bra. Reaching around her back, he unhooked the garment and let it fall to the floor, then leaned down and licked his way from the top of her breast down to the tip of one nipple, laving and nibbling before moving to the other one and giving it the same thorough treatment. She tipped her head back and moaned, her body shivering in delight.

He spent a good amount of time on the tight buds before she wrenched out of his grasp and shimmied the dress down and off, till it pooled at her feet. Then, her hot gaze on his, she hooked her thumbs into her barely there panties and got rid of them, too. Bared to him in every way, she was every dream he'd had come to life and more. Breasts not too large, just the right size for his hands, full with dusky nipples, red from his teasing. And her neatly trimmed pussy a treat for his eyes.

She reached out, fumbled with the button on his jeans with those trembling hands, causing him to take over. He unhooked, unzipped, and stripped them off, kicking them aside, unable to bear the clothing against his skin a minute longer, his boxer briefs going with them.

They were frantic for skin-on-skin contact, and as soon as he was naked, he backed her to the nearest wall and fused his lips to hers. He grasped her hips, gliding his hand upward until he cupped her firm breast. He massaged her nipple in his palm, then began to pull on the tip with his thumb and forefinger. She writhed against him, hooking her leg around his and grinding herself against his straining shaft.

Her pussy, hot and needy, rubbing into his cock was all he could take. "Bedroom," he said, breathing into her hair.

He grasped her hand and she led him to her room, a feminine place of yellows and white ruffles and pillows. Unable to wait, he picked her up and laid her on the bed, coming down over her, his cock nestled in her soft, heated flesh, pulsing and demanding to be allowed inside.

She arched her hips up, as if she could pull him into her by virtue of sheer need and desire alone.

"Not so fast," he said, pushing himself up and meeting her gaze. "I don't want this to be over before we even begin." And if he even felt a hint of her warm sex wrapped around his dick, that's exactly what would happen.

"It's torture, feeling you on my skin and not inside me, where I need you," she said, surprising him with her open, honest words.

"Then let me see what I can do to take the edge off." He slid between her legs, pushing her thighs apart with his hands. He took in her sweet pussy and lowered his head, swallowing a groan at the heady scent of her desire.

Parting her lips with his fingers, he dipped his head and began to feast on her damp sex. She moaned, her hands tangling his hair, pulling on the long strands as he teased and suckled her swollen flesh. He braced his hands on her thighs and brought her higher, licking and suckling her clit.

She yanked his hair harder and ground herself into him. He didn't let up, sliding his tongue inside her, while using his fingers to tease and play with her clit, wanting her to come and come hard before he took her in the most basic way.

His tongue darted into her, his fingers played, and suddenly she stiffened, yelled, and called out his name as she came, riding out her orgasm until the very end.

The sounds she made were sheer heaven, driving him insane.

Only when he was certain she was sated did he slide up her body, dragging his dick along her thigh and settling between her quivering legs so he could kiss her, letting her taste herself on his tongue.

His hips bucked of their own volition and he knew it was time. "Condom," he muttered. "Hang on." He eased off her, heading for his jeans. No, he hadn't planned it but he did have one shoved inside his wallet. It was old but not too ancient and it'd do the trick.

He ripped the foil packet and slid it over his aching cock. He glanced over to find her watching him with slumberous eyes, still hazy with desire. She lay against the bed, arms draped over her head, totally sated but her gaze focused intently on his dick in a way that made it stand at attention even more.

He placed one knee on the bed and came over her, cock poised and ready for action. He held himself in one hand and glided his cock over her swollen clit.

She moaned and met his gaze. "You have me ready again," she whispered.

"You'd better be, because this time you're coming around my cock, beautiful."

Her body flushed a sweet shade of pink.

Taking that as his signal, he lined himself up at her

entrance and drove deep.

"Kane!" She wrapped her legs around his waist and arched her hips into his.

"Fuck, you're so hot and tight."

Her fingernails dug into his shoulders at his words. "Move," she gritted out.

"My pleasure."

He pulled out, thrust back, beginning a rhythm she matched, her body clasping around his. Her fingers threaded through his hair, latching on. He pumped into her, harder with each consecutive plunge home, their hips grinding into each other, his dick hitting her pubic bone.

"God," she muttered, scoring her nails against his skin.

He took the pain, used it to drive him higher. He wasn't deep enough, needed more of her.

More.

Everything.

He pulled out.

"What?" she asked, surprised.

"Hang on." He flipped her over. "Knees," he instructed.

She scrambled onto all fours and he plunged into her. She screamed as his cock submerged completely.

Utter fucking bliss.

He wrapped an arm around her waist and began to

drive and grind, covering her with his body, owning her with the force of his need and desire. She groaned, arching her back, her hips meeting him thrust for thrust.

He cupped her breast in one hand, plucking and pulling at her nipple while taking her higher. Her guttural moans told him he was succeeding in bringing her to the same heights his body was reaching. It was raw, it was primal. It was unlike anything he'd experienced before and he doubted he ever would again.

Knowing he was close, he slid his hand lower, massaging her clit with his hand at the same time he braced himself for his own orgasm, his balls drawn up tight, as he forced himself to hold back until she came.

And she did, with a full-body spasm. "Kane, I'm coming. God, harder. I need it harder."

He slammed into her and she exploded beneath him, her entire being stiffening, then shuddering in release. He let go then, his climax overtaking him, mind and soul. He spurted into her over and over, losing what was left of his senses and his body inside this spectacular woman.

And when it was finished, she collapsed beneath him, falling to the mattress as he tumbled on top of her. Reality was far away as he struggled to catch his breath, but he knew he couldn't crush her much longer, so he pulled out and off her.

He felt the loss as he detached from her body and rolled to his side. He rose, got rid of the condom and returned to bed, pulling her into him as he struggled to return to his senses.

He wasn't sure how much time passed before a light giggle sounded beside him. "Halley?"

"That was spectacular," she murmured, pushing herself deeper into the cocoon of his body.

"Yes, it was." He wrapped an arm tighter around her because she wasn't pulling away and he took that as a huge win.

Then again, they'd agreed on great sex. They hadn't said as much, but taking things as they came pretty much defined casual to him. Not that anything he'd felt tonight had been casual.

He'd had his share of women and he'd had good sex. He'd never had blow-his-mind, off-the-charts, nobody-else-would-do sex before Halley. And something told him he never would again, so he'd better fucking find a way to keep her in his bed... and in his life.

Chapter Six

HALLEY WOKE UP earlier than Kane, but the fact that she'd slept while he was in her bed was a surprise. That she'd fallen asleep at all and remained out as long as she had, a bigger shock. No explanations about her insomnia needed, she thought in relief.

Lifting his arm off her body, she slipped out of bed, feeling sore in all the best possible ways. Her body wasn't used to sexual activity and she liked the feeling of knowing she'd been with Kane. And it had been incredible. It was one thing to be sexually compatible or to have an okay time in bed, another to practically have an out-of-body experience like she had last night.

She was wide awake with the overwhelming desire to express herself. So she dressed in an oversized tee shirt she often worked in because it fell to her knees, covering enough of her from paint splatter. Then she washed up and headed for her easel to work while the sun rose in the morning sky.

She was lost in her own world, she had no idea for how long, when she felt a hand on her shoulder.

"Hey," Kane said in a gruff, sexy morning voice.

She tilted her head back to meet his gaze and he treated her to a kiss on the lips. Her entire body sizzled at the touch of his mouth on hers.

"I like this," he said, hands in his jeans pockets as he gazed at the painting. "It's different from what you dropped off at the gallery this past weekend. Brighter, more… joyful."

She nodded, surprised he'd noticed, a warm feeling flooding her because he had. "Yes. I've seen a change in the last week or so." She shrugged because she couldn't pinpoint why, and placed her brush down. "Are you hungry?" Or was he in a rush to leave?

"I don't want to put you out. I can grab something on my way home. I want to shower, change, and grab some things before I come back to work on the deck."

She rose to her feet. "You're not putting me out. Let me feed you." She was hungry herself and surprisingly comfortable with him after last night. "I'm in the mood for French toast."

"Oh, my God, you could spoil a man."

She laughed. "It's a hazard for my figure but I can't help it. I love cooking."

He spun her around, pulling her against him.

"Your figure is perfect if you ask me."

"Thank you," she murmured.

He tugged her head back and kissed her hard, his tongue sliding past her lips. His hands slid up under her shirt, his palms landing on her waist, his calloused hands gliding up her skin until his fingers caressed the underside of her breast.

"Mmm," she said, rising up on her toes to kiss him more thoroughly.

"Not sure I need anything sweet for breakfast if I have you." He nipped at her lower lip.

Before she knew it, he'd scooped her up and carried her back to bed. "Kane!"

"What? Isn't this better than breakfast?" He teased her with another kiss and the thrust of his hips against hers.

Before they could get any further, the doorbell rang. She groaned.

"Expecting anyone?" he asked.

She shook her head as he rolled off her.

She glanced down at her bare legs, but she was covered enough, she supposed. She headed for the front door and looked through the peephole. She didn't recognize the woman outside, but a feeling of déjà vu stole through her, like she ought to know her or she'd met her before but just couldn't place her.

She was older than Halley, with light brown hair

that wasn't styled and hung long and straight around her face, no makeup, and she was drawn and tired-looking.

Again, that uneasy feeling crept through Halley. She knew but didn't want to face it. Wary, she opened the door. "Yes?"

"Halley?" the woman asked, almost expectantly.

She gripped the door harder. "Do I know you?" *You do*, a voice in her head whispered. *You know who it is.*

Her mouth ran dry.

"It's your mother."

Her knees almost buckled beneath her. Suspecting and being confronted by the truth were two different things. "Mom?" Her voice came out a croak.

"It's me, baby."

Halley remained frozen in place. "How did you find me?" she asked.

Her mother twisted her hands in front of her, her nerves showing as much as Halley's. "I looked you up."

"But I changed my last name," Halley said.

Her mother met her gaze. "I know. When I couldn't find you under your father's last name, Gifford, I thought about your aunt and how family-oriented she is. When I told her about you girls, she just wanted to bring you home and make you part of the family. So, I decided to take a chance and look under Ward."

She paused, wringing her hands, then said, "I admit I took your number from my sister." She looked down, embarrassed. "But you're my daughter and I wanted to speak to you. But I got nervous and hung up."

"So that was you," she murmured, staring at the woman in front of her who was a stranger... but wasn't.

She nodded. "Aren't you going to ask me to come in?"

From behind her, she heard Kane approach. She didn't know if she could handle this. Was it worse to do it in front of him or alone? she wondered, uncertain of the answer.

"Halley? Are you okay?" he asked.

She turned toward him and nodded. "It's my mother," she whispered.

Kane's eyes opened wide. He glanced over her shoulder at the woman waiting on the step. "Do you want me to leave you two alone?"

She shook her head, realizing she'd automatically answered her own question. She didn't want to do this by herself.

She pivoted back to her mother. "I'm sorry. Come in," she said, stepping back for her to enter.

Her mother was wearing a pair of old jeans and a beat-up sweatshirt. She looked tired and not at all like the fairy-tale version Halley had liked to make up when she was young and in foster care.

Her mother strode past Halley and stopped short when she saw Kane. "Who is this handsome man?" she asked.

Thank goodness he'd put his tee shirt on with his jeans, since he hadn't been wearing it earlier. Halley was uncomfortable with the way her mother was ogling Kane, as if she were looking her fill, no matter that he was younger.

"I'm Halley's boyfriend," Kane said, stepping up and wrapping an arm around her possessively. His body heat flowed into her along with strength she badly needed.

They might have agreed not to label themselves, but she had to admit she was grateful that Kane had stepped up and let her mother know someone was looking out for her. Just in case her mother was up to something like her aunt thought.

"So…" Halley wondered what her mother wanted. If she'd outright ask for money or—

"I thought we could talk."

Halley nodded. "Come into the family room," she murmured, gesturing toward the sofa in the big room where her easel sat in the corner.

"Hey." Kane pulled her back to him before she could follow her mother. "Are you sure you don't want to be alone with her?"

Despite having wanted a warm, bonding moment, Halley was still uncomfortable with the woman who'd given birth to her. "If you don't mind staying? I don't want to put you in an awkward position, though, so if you want to go—"

"If you want me, I'm here." He squeezed her hand, then waited for her to be ready to head into the room where her mother waited.

She drew a deep breath and walked toward the family room, Kane at her back.

They settled on the sofa. Her mother had chosen a chair nearby.

"Look at you, all grown up," her mother murmured.

Halley blushed, not knowing what to say.

"And this house is beautiful." Her mother rose and walked toward the sliding glass doors overlooking the beach. "Look at that view." She stared out at the ocean for a few long seconds before turning around and reseating herself on the chair. "So tell me about yourself," she said.

"Well, I paint." Halley gestured to the easel where her current work sat.

"Oh! I'd love to see!" Jumping up, her mother

walked over to her small painting area. "Oh, beautiful! I love the colors."

Halley smiled. "Thank you. My work is displayed in the gallery in town."

Her mother clasped her hands together. "That's wonderful."

"How have you been?" Halley asked.

Her mother sobered, her expression less pleased than before. "It's been difficult," she said. "Adjusting to life and looking for work."

"I can imagine," Kane said.

"But you're managing?" Halley asked, concerned.

"Well…" Her mother started to speak, then seemed to change her mind, shaking her head. "I'm fine. I do wish your sister would see me, but she seems to feel the same way your aunt does. That I haven't changed. That I'm only out for myself and that I'll fall back into my old ways." She shifted uncomfortably on the sofa.

"And will you?" Halley asked.

Her mother swallowed hard. "I'd like to think not. And I appreciate you seeing me. Giving me a chance."

Halley wasn't sure what this was, a beginning, maybe. So far her mother hadn't given any indication that she wanted something from her, so she was hopeful for a relationship with her going forward.

"I should let you go. I just wanted to… see you."

Her mother rose to her feet.

Halley and Kane followed. He'd been mostly silent through the visit, but his quiet support meant the world to her.

She walked her mother to the door. "Thanks for coming by."

"I'll be in touch," her mother said.

Halley shut the door behind her and turned to Kane, sagging against the wall. "Well, that wasn't too awkward," she said sarcastically.

He shot her a sympathetic glance. "You have to start somewhere."

She nodded. "I wonder if I'll hear from her again soon."

"You'll see. She didn't give you a way to contact her, so the ball's in her court."

"True." She straightened and walked into the kitchen. "So... breakfast?" she asked, forcing cheer.

In reality she was exhausted from that brief visit and needed time to process having seen her mother for the first time in what felt like forever.

"Listen, I think I'm going to get going," he said, stroking his knuckles down her cheek. "I'll be back later to work, and in the meantime, you can think about what all this means to you."

She reacted to his caress, her nipples tightening, her body swaying toward his, but he was right. As usual, he sensed what she needed and she was grateful.

"Before I go, I was wondering. Do you want to go to the festival in town next weekend?"

Halley knew the annual event was a combination of things. Rosewood's vendors, like the florist and the bakery, and the clothing and other shops, would take their wares outside and sell from individual booths. It also involved carnival-like treats brought in by the town for a get-together that attracted locals and tourists alike.

Halley didn't make a habit of going because of the large crowds, but she was hoping to get her newest work to Faith for display there. The project had been on the back burner for a long time. Halley had always known something was missing, but it was only lately, when she'd brought brighter colors into her work, that she realized how to make the canvas pop for the viewer. A short week and she'd finished a project that had been sitting for six months.

Glaziers had a catalogue of their paintings, and Faith had promised to include anything new Halley had. She could drop it off in a few days after it dried.

"Halley?"

"I hadn't planned on going but—"

"But you'll go with me," he said, ending her sentence for her.

She studied his handsome face. She didn't want to

disappoint him, and she was happy he'd asked her to join him. She could push past her insecurities for one day. "Okay."

Pleasure lit his expression. "Okay, we'll discuss plans closer to the day. Now I'm really going to head home, shower, and come back to work."

She started forward, intending to walk him out, but he hooked an arm around her waist, pulling her against him.

"Uh-uh. You don't get rid of me without a proper good-bye." His eyes blazed with sudden heat and her body responded in kind.

He had that effect on her. All he needed to do was give her *that look* and she was melting. "What did you have in mind?" she asked, her voice a purr.

He dipped his head and pressed his lips to hers, the kiss going from zero to sixty in an instant. She parted her lips and he slipped his tongue inside. There was nothing tame about the way he took her mouth, devouring her and letting her know in no uncertain terms, he was claiming her. And by the time he lifted his head and came up for air, she was panting, not just out of breath but with very basic need.

He swiped his thumb over his damp lips. "Now that's a proper good-bye." He winked and released her, then strode to the door and let himself out, leaving her with shaky legs and desire pulsing through her veins.

✧   ✧   ✧

HALLEY WAS WATERING her plants outside her front door. The carnations were in full bloom and beautiful red colors exploded on her porch. She wasn't sure the flowers warranted a watering since she'd done this yesterday, but she needed the distraction from the myriad thoughts running through her mind.

Phoebe had called a little while ago and she wanted to talk, which meant Halley was going to have to tell her she'd seen their mother. And Halley wanted to have a conversation with Aunt Joy about her mom. Because the woman Halley had talked to hadn't seemed to want anything other than a chance to get to know her daughter.

Which was exactly what Halley had desired, too. So why did she feel so uneasy now? She couldn't place the discomfort, but it remained when she thought about her wayward parent.

She refocused on her flowers and had just finished up when a white car pulled up and parked on the street parallel to her house. Kane's sister exited the vehicle with a foil-wrapped bundle in her hands.

Halley placed the watering can out front as Andrea approached. "Hi."

"Hi," the other woman said when she reached Halley. Andrea joined her on the porch, dressed as casually as Halley in a pair of jeans and a loose-fitting top.

"To what do I owe this visit?"

Andrea smiled, extending the item in her hands. "For one thing, I'm returning your plate. And for another, I wanted to apologize. Our family dinners can get loud, but last night we aired private business. That was rude and I'm sure it made you uncomfortable." She held out the covered plate. "We ate your cookies last night. My boy can really devour them. But I made some sugar cookies for you to say I'm sorry."

Halley accepted the plate. "Thank you, Andrea."

"Call me Andi, please."

She smiled. "Andi, that was thoughtful but I promise you, it's fine. Nobody understands a little dysfunction more than me." Especially after the visit from her mother.

Andi studied her intently. "I appreciate it, and if you don't mind me saying so, I get why Kane is so interested in you. And trust me, my brother doesn't get invested often."

Was Kane invested? And did she want him to be? They were taking it one day at a time, no expectations, no labels. He'd even been the one to suggest it was okay to be casual.

Before she could respond, Andi went on. "You're

so kind and sensitive. Anyway, that's it. I wanted to make things right for Kane in case you were upset."

"Not at all. Umm… Do you want to come inside? Have a cold drink?" she offered.

"Sure!"

Andi eagerly followed her inside. And an hour later, she'd had her first girl time with anyone other than her sister, talking about things from who cut her hair and did her highlights to their favorite television shows to binge—Halley wasn't a big binger but Andi had talked her into trying some of her favorites. They discussed sharing cooking recipes and Andi told her funny stories about raising a boy. Apparently her son was obsessed with his weiner.

By the time Andi went home, Halley was left with the odd feeling that she'd made a friend. She was a little dizzy from the woman's friendly demeanor and bubbly personality, and overwhelmed since she didn't usually do girl bonding. True, she had her sister, but never in her life had she made a true friend. It was odd since her treatment by girls in her past, both in foster care and when she'd gone to high school here afterwards, made her wary. Andi, like her brother, was different. She was genuine.

For Halley, having a real friend was going to take some getting used to.

✧   ✧   ✧

OVER THE REST of the week, Kane fell into a set pattern. He would work his normal hours at the garage, and on days it didn't rain, he would show up for a few hours of work on Halley's house. The deck was coming along at an expectedly slow pace with one man doing the work.

Most nights he worked, she cooked dinner, giving him a chance to spend time with her and glean more insight into who she was as a person. She loved cooking shows, which was to his benefit, didn't watch much television because she'd rather be painting, and she enjoyed reading romance novels. He'd cracked her shell, at least to the point where he could get her to laugh easily and often, which made his fucking day.

Sex wasn't part of the equation, not because he didn't want her, because he fucking did, but he didn't want her to think he was using her because he had easy access thanks to his work on her house. And also because he wanted her to have time to think about him, want him, and miss what they'd shared that one time they'd been intimate.

Sex with Halley consumed his thoughts because she'd been so open and eager, surprisingly so considering her hesitance to get involved in a serious relationship. He figured that she'd been telling herself their situation was casual, but there had been nothing casual about how they came together. They fit in a way not all couples did in bed, and he wondered if she realized they had something special.

During their times together these last weeks, she'd kept their conversations casual, not delving deep into her past in foster care or anything else, for that matter. And he still wondered what was behind the walls she guarded. The one thing he knew for certain, he wasn't finished figuring her out.

The Sunday of the festival, he picked her up at ten a.m. She greeted him at the door and shocked him with her outfit. Instead of wearing her usual flirty dress, she chose a flirty denim skirt with a ruffle that was short enough to showcase her long legs, a tucked-in bright purple tank top that gave him an enticing look at her full breasts but remained classy, and a pair of white Chucks on her feet.

Her hair was pulled into a ponytail and her sunglasses were perched on top of her head. She appeared young, flirty, and happy, a look that was fairly new. When he'd come upon her on the road alongside her broken-down car, she'd been much more withdrawn and wary.

He hadn't seen this excitement in her eyes before and he liked the change. "Looking forward to today?" he asked.

"I wouldn't have thought so, but you've talked it up so much I actually am."

"Good. We'll have fun. Are you ready?" he asked, extending his hand.

"Ready." She slowly reached out and accepted it, her smaller hand soft and delicate as she curled her fingers around his palm.

His skin burned and his cock jumped behind the denim of his jeans. Not the time, he told himself, counting down from ten and concentrating on the numbers, not her sexy self.

They drove the short distance and he parked on the outskirts of town. Together, they walked in comfortable silence toward the fair.

She didn't argue when he grabbed her hand again, and he was proud to have her on his arm. It had been years since he'd shown up in town with a woman on his arm, and the last one had humiliated him spectacularly. He'd overheard her talking to a friend and she'd humiliated him in that conversation. Her comments had bruised his ego, and at the time, he'd thought she'd hurt his heart.

Only with distance had he realized that he'd been more infatuated with Liza than anything else. Still, it had caused him to pull back and be very wary of who he took to his bed. Local women who didn't want much had worked well for his busy life and schedule. Until Halley.

"So what's the plan?" she asked as the high white

tents came into view.

"We'll check out the booths and eat lots of sugary treats. I've been going to this fair since I was a little kid. I can vouch for the funnel cakes and the cotton candy."

She grinned. "I can get behind that."

They strode past various vendors, stopping when he saw someone he knew, which was often. Andi was working a food booth for the Blue Wall, Nicky by her side.

"Hey, guys! This morning I can offer you French toast sticks, and if you come back after lunch I'll have sliders," Andi said, a big grin on her face.

"They're awesome!" Nicky said, bouncing up and down with excitement. "Mom said if I help her serve food, I can go look at the puppies later."

"Puppies?" Halley asked, her voice perking up.

Andi pushed two plates with French toast sticks on them across the table. "Nicky, give Uncle Kane and Halley a napkin, please."

"Here, Uncle Kane." He slapped napkins down on the table.

Halley looked at the little boy. "Thank you," she said. "You're a great helper."

"Puppies," Kane noted to Halley. "That would keep any child happy."

She turned and looked up at him with wide eyes.

"Puppies," she whispered, her voice exuding excitement.

He wrapped his arms around her waist and pulled her toward him, burying his face in the back of her hair and taking a long breath in. She smelled of strawberry shampoo, and his groin tightened immediately. "I take it you want to go see the shelter stand?"

Her grin was the only answer he needed. He called to his sister to hang on to the food until later, took Halley's hand, and headed in the direction of the puppies.

HALLEY WAS HAVING a blast. So far, their day had been a far cry from the intense people-filled nightmare she'd envisioned. She could handle crowds; she just didn't like individuals getting close enough to rub up against her or touch her in any way that felt like a violation. So far, so good. Besides, she had Kane beside her and that made up for any discomfort she might feel.

They approached the local shelter's area, her heart racing with anticipation.

"Are you just excited to see the dogs or are you really interested in adoption?" he asked.

The truth was, this was a spur-of-the-moment decision, but the minute Andi had mentioned that the puppies were here courtesy of the local shelter, that they were abandoned dogs who needed a home, her heart had been engaged.

"I hadn't considered it until now but I love dogs. One of the homes I lived in had a black lab. He was so soft and gentle. He used to sleep beside me. I missed him when I left." Since this had been before her last home, where that awful night had happened, she'd slept well, especially with Blackie by her side.

He tugged on her hand and they stopped walking. "Why did you leave that home?" he asked.

She swallowed hard. "One of the girls there accused me of stealing money she had stashed away. She lied. I wouldn't take something that didn't belong to me, but she carried on so much Mrs. B believed her." She remembered how devastated she'd been because that had been one of the good homes she lived in.

She'd gone from there to the house where the woman in charge had a perv of a husband, and that had been a nightmare.

Kane squeezed her hand in reassurance. "I know you'd never steal. And I'm sorry you had to go through that."

"Oh, that was a piece of cake compared to what came later." Her eyes flew open wide as she realized what she'd just said.

"Halley? What—"

Before he could finish his question, someone bumped into her, jostling her side and sending her sprawling against Kane.

He grasped her arms and kept her steady. The same couldn't be said for her rapidly beating heart. Between that trip into the past, her never faraway memories of *him*, and now someone pushing her, her throat was full and she was near tears.

"Hey." Kane spoke softly. "Are you okay?" he asked, obviously concerned.

She managed a nod. "Can we just go see the dogs?" Burying her face in soft fur was exactly what she needed right now.

He studied her for a long while. "Okay. Puppies it is." He still looked worried but he was obviously more concerned with keeping her calm.

They approached the booth and disappointment filled her. "There are so many people there," she said, wondering how they'd get close with all the kids crowding the area with the dogs.

"I'm sure they're not all legitimately interested in adopting. You are. We'll get you up front," he promised.

True to his word, he maneuvered them to the side of the booth and around the edge of the table, where he flagged down a volunteer. "We'd like to see the dogs," he said to the young woman with a purple stripe in her hair. "We're interested in adoption." He glanced at Halley. "Well, she is."

"Sure thing! Can you tell me if you're interested in any specific kind of dog? Big? Small?"

Halley ran her tongue over her dry lips. "I want an easy personality. The kind that could be like an... emotional support dog," she said, forcing the words past her tight throat.

The idea had come to her when she'd been talking about Blackie. Maybe getting a dog wouldn't only be fun but it would help her sleep at night because she wouldn't be alone.

"Be right back!" the girl said.

Halley looked up at Kane. "It's not that I need the help but I—"

"You don't owe me an explanation, beautiful. You need a dog in your life, period. I think it'll be great for you."

She smiled. "Yeah. Me, too. I'll take it for walks on the beach and runs in the water."

"He or she can sleep with you in bed and keep you company." He leaned in and kissed her nose. "Except when I'm there. Then he or she is going to have to move aside."

She laughed, almost relieved, because for the last week, he hadn't made a move. Yes, he'd been present and interested, there'd been a lot of hugging and touching and brief kisses, but she'd honestly been left wondering why he wasn't taking her in his arms and to bed. Instead he'd left her sexually frustrated each night when he said good-night, kissed her lips, and left her to climb beneath the sheets alone.

"Here we go. This is Monty." The woman held out a fluffy dog with huge sad eyes, a gleaming black coat, and the sweetest look on his face.

Halley reached out and took him in her arms. "Hey, Monty. What's your story, you sweet boy?"

"He was found abandoned in the park by someone who brought him to the shelter. It was winter and he was cold and matted, dirty, and so afraid," the girl, whose name tag read Lyndie, said. "Then Gail, the woman who is in charge of the shelter, took him home to foster him."

At the word *foster*, Halley felt an immediate kinship with the dog. He'd been abandoned and left alone, much like she'd been. And he'd gone to a home where someone had taken him in and cared for him. Halley hadn't found love in her foster homes, but a couple of them had made her feel safe... until they hadn't. This puppy would be giving her unconditional love and devotion, and she wanted to give him a safe haven in return. For the rest of his life.

"He's come a long way," Lyndie went on. "And she's had him certified as an emotional support animal.

Gail has been waiting for the right home for him."

Kane reached out and petted the top of his soft head.

Lyndie glanced over to where people were calling her name. "Listen, take him behind me, where there's a quiet stretch of grass. Get to know him now, and if you think he's right for you, come by the shelter tomorrow. You can fill out the paperwork, meet Gail, and hopefully you'll be his new home."

Halley met Kane's gaze. "Do we have time?"

He nodded. "All the time in the world," he assured her.

For the next half hour, she discovered Monty knew how to sit, lie down, and give her his paw. He also enjoyed snuggles, which he let her know he wanted by butting his head against her stomach.

"I love him already," she whispered, looking up at Kane.

He laughed. "I take it a trip to the shelter is in your plans for tomorrow?"

"First thing." Her stomach flipped in excitement.

She cuddled Monty one last time and kissed his fluffy head before giving him back to Lyndie, promising she'd come by in the morning.

"Well, that was a success," Kane said, clasping her hand in his. "Are you hungry yet?"

She nodded.

"French toast or funnel cakes?" he asked.

She wrinkled her nose in thought. "French toast."

They started back to Andi's booth when a female voice called Kane's name. He didn't turn right away, so the woman called again.

"Kane!"

He released her hand and spun around at the same time a tall, willowy brunette in sky-high heels and obviously expensive jeans and an over-the-top blouse walked right up to him and wrapped her arms around his neck.

"It's so good to see you!" She pressed her body against him, visibly rubbing her breasts against his chest.

Jealousy rose to the surface, green and ugly. Hadn't this woman seen him holding hands with Halley before she attached herself to him like a leech? More likely she just didn't care. Who was she to Kane? Halley wondered, the urge to pull her long hair out by the roots strong.

He grasped the woman's arms and pulled her off him. "Liza, what the hell are you doing?"

"Saying hello, sugar. I've missed you and I planned on looking you up."

He scowled, an expression Halley had never seen on him before, turning his normally easygoing look to hard granite. "Doubtful since summer's over," he muttered. "If you're looking for another fling with the mechanic, you're out of luck."

"He's taken," Halley said, stepping up and hooking her arm through his.

Kane grinned. "What she said."

Liza's mouth dropped open, as if unable to believe he'd turn her down. "Jesus, Kane, you know you've never had better than me."

He burst out laughing. "Keep telling yourself that, *sugar*," he said in a saccharine-sweet tone, clearly meant to mock her.

With that, he turned and walked away, pulling Halley along with him.

"What was that about?" she asked as they headed in the opposite direction.

Kane let out a low groan. "Can it wait until we're alone?" he asked.

She nodded, curious about the woman but willing to respect what he needed. He always did the same for her.

His hand around her waist, he led her back to his sister. "Hey, Andi."

"Hi, you two. Any dog success?" she asked.

"Maybe," Halley said. "Well, make that I hope so. The shelter owner has to approve me, so I'll know more tomorrow." She held up two fingers and crossed them.

Andi grinned. "If I bring Nicky over to see your dog, maybe that'll do for a while. He keeps begging for a puppy, but I work so many hours and I don't want to rely on Dad for help."

"Where is Nicky?" Halley asked.

"He's walking around with a friend whose mom took charge of them."

"And Dad, how is he?" Kane asked. "I mean, I know how he is at work—surly and obnoxious—which leads me to believe he's finding games, online or otherwise, and losing." He glanced at his sister for confirmation.

Halley followed along in silence, not wanting to intrude on a conversation that was deeply personal and very difficult.

"Honestly, he's not good. He stays out late or he's holed up in the office on the computer. I think he's learned to clear the browser from one of his friends, because I haven't caught him that way." She frowned as she explained.

"What's he doing for money?" he asked.

"Isn't that always the question. We stopped loaning him anything a long time ago and he stopped asking. He did have that poker windfall and I have no idea how much they played for. He has the money you pay him for working… I've been paying the mortgage and expenses."

"Jesus, Andi—"

She held up a hand before Kane could jump in with an argument. "Don't you think I know? But it's exhausting to try and budget him or take his money from him on payday. It's easier for me to just live my life, you know?"

The house was the one Kane grew up in, he'd told her as much over dinner one night. She also knew it had a second mortgage.

"I get it," he muttered. "And I'm sorry you're dealing with it on a more personal level."

"It's fine. I'm managing. Between my job at the Blue Wall and working at the flower shop during the day, I'm making ends meet with room for some extras."

"Okay but if you need anything…"

"I know. You're here. And thank you." She leaned across the table and kissed his cheek. "Now can I feed you two?"

Halley's stomach chose that moment to grumble. It wasn't too noisy for anyone else to hear but she felt it intensely. "I'm starving," she said.

Andi happily served them again. "So was that Liza I saw attacking you earlier?" Andi asked, as Halley nibbled at the sweetest, lightest French toast she'd ever eaten. It had a slight crunch and was delicious.

She glanced at Kane, whose face took on that same

scowl. "The woman is insane. She acted like she thought we could pick up where we left off three years ago. She's out of her mind."

Andi laughed. "Well, it looked like you set her straight. After you left, she stomped off in those high heels with her nose in the air. Good riddance," she muttered.

Halley's curiosity was through the roof. She hated thinking of that woman in bed with Kane. It turned her stomach. But they both had pasts and she couldn't hold Liza against him. Obviously, it hadn't ended well, because every time her name came up, he looked like he'd eaten something nasty.

They might not have a defined relationship, but it hurt to think of him with someone else, just the same.

Chapter Seven

THE SIGHT OF Halley and that puppy had hit Kane hard. She'd obviously fallen for the poor, abandoned dog because she could relate to him, somehow. He'd seen her eyes when Lyndie had mentioned he'd been cold and frightened, then taken in and fostered temporarily. The situation had hit home and his heart hurt for all she'd lived through.

He might have issues with his father, but he'd always had a parent and a roof over his head he knew was safe, that he could trust. Something had obviously happened to Halley in one of those foster homes. She'd said the one where she'd been accused of stealing and thrown out had been a picnic compared to one of the others. Just what was she holding inside? And how could he get her to talk about it and unburden herself?

He glanced at her profile as they drove home in comfortable silence, the windows down on his Camaro. The scent of the ocean drifted into the confines of the car, a salty, warm smell he associated with home, and thanks to the hours he spent working on the deck, he now associated the ocean scent with Halley, as well.

He parked in front of her house and walked with her up the driveway and path. She let them inside and looked around.

"I'm going to have to dog proof this place," she murmured. "Make sure no plants are on the floor or within reach and check for small pieces or things Monty could get into."

"Yes, you will. But it sounded like he's well trained so I think you lucked out."

She walked into the kitchen and tossed her keys on the counter. "I'm excited."

He grinned. "Can't say I blame you."

Her phone chimed from inside her purse. She took it off her shoulder and dug inside to pull out her cell. She glanced at the caller name and hit End.

"Nothing important?" he asked.

She met his gaze. "My mom," she said.

He raised his eyebrows in surprise. In the last couple of weeks, she hadn't mentioned hearing from her mother. "Is this the first time she's called since the day she came over?"

Halley shook her head. "She's been calling every few days. We've been talking and catching up." Her cheeks flushed pink.

"You can tell me, you know. I won't judge you for wanting a relationship with your mother."

"Even though she was a drug addict and abandoned me when I was practically a baby?" She looked at him with wide, blue, concerned eyes.

He grasped her hands in front of them. "She's your mother. If you need to give her a chance, then that's what you do. I certainly can understand that."

She swallowed hard and smiled, her shoulders relaxing at his words.

He was almost afraid to ask but decided to jump in. "Have you told your aunt and your sister you've seen her or spoken with her?"

She shook her head. "I want to. I even planned to but I chickened out. I'm nervous." She bit down on her lower lip. "I know Phoebe will see it as a betrayal and Aunt Joy will work herself up worrying."

"I get it but you're an adult. You can do what you want. What you need or makes you happy."

"You amaze me," she murmured.

"Why is that?"

"Because you get me in ways nobody else does. Not even my family and they're the closest people to me."

He was glad she recognized how well they clicked and not just in bed. "I want to be the one to chase away your demons. You can trust me to be there when you need me. And when you don't." He lifted a hand and cupped her cheek in his palm, stroking the smooth skin with his thumb.

"I want to believe you," she whispered and tipped her head into the cup of his hand.

"Then do." He slowly lowered his head until his mouth brushed hers.

Once, twice, three times he glided his lips across hers, deliberately gentle and coaxing until she parted, opening for him. His tongue slipped past her lips, tangling with hers. A soft moan escaped her throat, and he slid his hand from her chin to the back of her head, angling her for better, deeper access. She tasted sweet, and he stroked the inside of her mouth and her tongue with his own.

"Bed," she whispered, arching her body and pressing her breasts into his chest.

He lifted her into his arms and strode into her bedroom, gently laying her down on the bed. Not waiting, she slid her skirt over her hips and down her long legs, taking her panties along with it, kicking them both aside.

While his gaze came to rest on her sex, she arched her back and removed her shirt, tossing it onto the floor. A flick of her wrist and her bra went next. She'd kicked her shoes off at the door and now lay naked, splayed out like a goddess before him.

Her gorgeous breasts tempted him, dusky nipples made for his mouth. Her damp sex beckoned to be filled. He sucked in a shallow breath, his body eager to join her.

He kicked off his shoes, then quickly pulled out the condom he'd stuffed into his pocket earlier, knowing his patience with waiting was wearing thin. He shucked his jeans and tee shirt and stood, his cock erect and ready.

"See what you do to me?" he asked, gripping his shaft with his hand, pumping up and down in two swift strokes, his blood boiling with need.

Her eyes dilated, her pupils huge as her gaze zeroed in on his dick.

He ripped the condom open with his teeth and slid it onto his straining shaft before joining her on the bed, gliding his erection over her bared sex as his body came down over hers.

She moaned at the intimate contact, arching her hips grinding her pussy against his cock. He gritted his teeth and held back a groan of his own.

He leaned down and suckled her nipple, teasing, toying, pulling it between his teeth. When she gasped and moaned, he soothed the distended bud with his tongue, lapping where he'd lightly bitten, licking around her soft skin.

Her fingers came to his hair, pulling hard. "Now, Kane. I need you know."

Unable to wait and knowing she didn't want or need him to, he braced his hands on the mattress and raised himself over her. Gripping his cock in one hand, he teased her clit with his erection, gliding the head over the tight bundle of nerves until she was writhing with need.

"Kane, please." She begged him again, and it would be his pleasure to give her what she wanted. He notched himself at her entrance. "Ready, beautiful?"

She nodded, her hooded eyes hazy with desire. Then he slid home, burying himself inside her warm, wet heat. He clenched his teeth, focusing on not coming right then. Instead he focused on her pleasure, sliding out slowly and thrusting back in deep.

She moaned, lifting her legs, arching her hips and pulling him in as far as he could go, her inner walls clenching around his cock. His body shook, and sweat broke out on his forehead and back, the searing heat bringing him closer to climax.

This woman meant more to him than he could or was willing to express, and the more he got to know her, the deeper he fell under her spell. It was fast but he'd never *felt* this much before.

He needed to see her looking at him, to note the look on her face as he took her higher. "Eyes on me," he said and she forced her heavy eyelids open, those blue eyes focusing on his.

He ground himself into her and began a steady rhythm of pumping in and out, watching the rapturous expression on her face as she climbed higher. Sliding his hands up her body, he captured her hands in his, holding her wrists tight in his grasp.

Suddenly she stiffened and cried out, her orgasm triggering his own release, an incredible soaring, as he lost himself completely.

Afterwards, once they'd caught their breath and he'd cleaned up, he lay against the headboard, Halley's head against his chest, her body aligned with his. Her steady breathing soothed him as he tangled his fingers in her hair and played with the long strands.

"So are you going to tell me about Liza?" she asked, her fingers tracing patterns on his chest. Her soft touch felt good and was making his dick perk up again.

Liza wasn't a subject he wanted to get into while lying in bed with Halley... but he would because she'd asked. "We were involved a few summers ago. She was renting a house similar to yours on the other side of the bay. She brought her car into the shop and set her sights on me immediately." He expelled a rough breath.

Thinking back, he could see the manipulation

she'd used from the minute they'd met, but embarrassingly he'd been blind to it at the time. She was beautiful in what he now thought was a fake kind of way, but he'd been attracted to her and she'd played him well.

"She convinced me she was interested in something long term, which I now know was her way of keeping me in her bed for the duration of the summer. I'm not exactly proud of how I was taken in by her."

"What happened?" Halley asked.

"I overheard her talking to her friend the same day I'd planned to discuss with her how we were going to keep seeing each other after the summer ended. Liza was saying that she couldn't wait to go home at the end of the week. That I was great in bed but being with a mechanic was getting old. She was ready to hang out at the bars where she could meet a Wall Street guy or investment banker she could marry. Who could take her to nice places because Rosewood's offerings were slim pickings compared to Manhattan."

"Ouch." Halley pushed herself up and slid on top of him, meeting his gaze. "Her loss," she murmured, placing a kiss on his lips. "And my gain."

He slid his hand into her nape and held her in place, kissing her hard and deep.

When he broke the kiss, she wriggled her hips. "Ready to go again?" she asked. She came to a sitting position on his waist and raised herself up, poised so she could take him inside her body.

"Condom," he said, though he hated that word as it passed his lips. He wanted to feel her bare walls around his cock.

"I'm on the pill. It's been a very long time for me and I've had yearly exams. I'm good if you are." She offered him his wildest dream come true.

"I'm clean, too. Tested yearly and recently," he assured her.

In reply, she gripped his cock in her hand and slid down on top of him. He groaned as her body stretched to accommodate his width and closed his eyes in utter bliss when he was sheathed completely.

"Eyes on me," she said, and when he opened his eyes, she was grinning.

His own laugh was cut short when she began to move, riding him, gliding up and down, clasping herself around his shaft.

He reached out and cupped her breasts in his hands, molding and kneading them. A throaty groan escaped her throat. His cock pulsed at the sexy sound. His balls were drawn up tight, his climax not far away.

He pinched her nipples with his fingertips, rubbing the tight buds between his thumb and forefinger, nearly coming apart when she clenched tightly around him in response. With every downward slide, her hips rolled forward and she gasped, telling him she was close to coming, as well.

He wanted to flip her and pound into her, but he also got off on watching her make herself come around his cock.

Up, down, forward, grind. Up, down, forward, grind. She repeated the motions until her head tipped back and she came on a slow moan.

"God, Kane. So good. So good," she chanted as she let go, the glorious look on her face a sight to behold.

Somehow he waited until she was finished, until every last contraction had rocked through her, before he began to buck up into her. He held on to her hips and slammed her down on top of him.

Without warning, she began to tremble again, and as he came hard, his entire being taken on an explosive ride, she screamed and rode out another orgasm beneath him.

✧   ✧   ✧

KANE MUST HAVE drifted off to sleep, because he was startled awake when Halley hit him with a flailing arm. It was still daylight and the clock read five p.m. They must have been exhausted from the festival to pass out in the afternoon.

When Halley hit him again, he rolled over to find

her asleep but thrashing back and forth in bed. "No." She smacked at the air with her arms.

"Halley," he whispered, but she didn't wake up. He nudged her arm gently and continued to call her name, louder this time.

"What?" She woke with a jolt, her eyes focusing slowly on his.

"Are you okay?" he asked in a gentle voice because she looked frightened and her body still trembled. He couldn't yet tell if she wanted to be held, so he waited for now.

She drew her tongue over her lips and gave him a short nod. "Yeah. I'm fine."

But she curled into a fetal position and he called bullshit. She was nowhere near fine. "You can talk to me, you know. I told you earlier, I'll never judge."

She shook her head furiously. "I can't."

He narrowed his gaze. "Why not? Get it out and you'll feel better." He hoped. She'd obviously worked herself into a state and was holding something terrible inside.

She curled further into herself. "I can't talk about it, Kane. Not to you, not to anyone. I can't even bring myself to say the words out loud," she said, her voice cracking.

He didn't wait for permission and pulled her into the safety of his arms. She stiffened, then relaxed, accepting the comfort. She released the hold she had on her tight muscles and wound her body around his instead of the little ball she'd contorted herself into.

"Whatever it is, it has power over you and you need to let it go." He had a hunch and decided to push. "Is this about that foster home you mentioned?"

She nodded into his chest.

What could have her so traumatized? he wondered, then froze in horror at the thought that ran through his brain. "Halley, were you raped?" He nearly choked over the word, his entire body rejecting the idea.

She must have heard the panic in his voice, because she rushed to reassure him. "No. Not that."

Then what? he wondered. "Let it out," he urged her again.

Rolling to her side, she didn't stop trembling but she did begin to speak. "I was thirteen and in the last foster home before my aunt found me. The one after the place that accused me of stealing."

He began to stroke her back. Slow, steady, reassuring strokes.

"They were a married couple, Elsa and Ray Cartman. And I was never comfortable there. From the first day, I didn't like how Ray looked at me."

Nervous and a little queasy, he wrapped his arms around her while she spoke.

"For a while, that's all it was. Uncomfortable. But

about a month before I left, I woke up one night because something felt wrong. I opened my eyes and Ray was standing over me." A shudder went through her. "When he realized I was awake, he left. After that, he made it a habit of standing over me at night, so I stopped sleeping. I kept a light on in the room from that time on."

He exhaled a long breath. He could understand how that would be traumatizing for a thirteen-year-old and even cause nightmares, but at least—

"It gets worse," she said, surprising him. He'd thought, or at least he'd hoped, that had been the whole story.

"Go on," he whispered in a rough voice.

"I… He… I woke up one night and he had unzipped his pants and pulled them down. He was stroking himself, masturbating while I slept. And before I could scream, he came on my bed, on me while I lay there," she said, shaking like a leaf and rushing out the words as if expelling them would make them not as bad.

"Oh, baby." He held her tight, rocking her into him even as nausea filled him and he had to hold back a gag. For her sake, he needed to be strong. After all, he was the one who'd forced her to relive this. "What happened next?" he asked softly.

"I screamed. Elsa came running. She blamed me

for teasing him, tempting him to sin."

Kane curled his hands into fists, then released them before she could notice. The last thing she needed was his anger. "Were you moved again?"

"Would you believe social services came the next day? My aunt had contacted them, looking for me. A day too late. Or a lifetime," she muttered, breaking down in tears.

He couldn't do anything except hold her as she cried, so he did, understanding, at last, why she had walls, why she didn't like people, and why she preferred to keep to herself. Which made the fact that he'd gotten in a true miracle. One he wouldn't take for granted.

✧   ✧   ✧

HALLEY WAS SHAKY for the rest of the night. Kane hadn't wanted to leave. In fact, he'd insisted on staying but she'd forced him to go. Sunday was dinner with his sister, father, and nephew, and she didn't want him to miss his routine with his family. Though he claimed they were just bringing in pizza after the long day at the fair, she'd been firm. He needed to leave. Because she needed to prove to herself that she was strong enough to face her demons and handle them alone.

Kane was a good man and he'd been there for her in many ways, but it hadn't changed her desire to rely on herself. To not trust in anyone too completely because she'd only ever been on her own.

Flashlight in hand and alone in the dark, she walked down the beach, letting her toes dip into the water. She listened to the roar of the waves and allowed peace to wash over her.

The past was behind her, she told herself. She had a good life. She had her sister and her aunt. Her mother seemed to be honestly repentant and wanted a relationship, which pleased her so much. When the time was right, she could even ask her mother what had happened to her baby sister, Juliette. Was it possible to locate her now? Hope trickled through her at the thought.

But for now, things were on an upswing. She hopefully had a dog coming home tomorrow. And she had a man in her life who understood her, and right now that was enough.

It had to be. No matter how much she was coming to feel for Kane, trust was something she didn't think she had inside her. Not for the long haul, and he deserved so much more than she was capable of giving.

✧   ✧   ✧

EARLY MONDAY MORNING, Halley had shaken off the effects of yesterday's trip into the past. She hadn't slept well, but she hadn't had a nightmare, either.

Maybe Kane was right. Getting it out had helped. She hadn't talked about that awful night since the therapist her aunt had made her see when she came home. Those visits had given her tools to pack the past away, and though she hadn't done it one hundred percent successfully, she was coping day by day.

She arrived at the shelter, eager to meet Gail and hopefully finalize a doggie adoption. She needed Monty more than ever, something she realized as she'd tossed and turned last night. She prayed Gail found her to be a suitable home for him.

Once there, she walked inside and found Lyndie behind the desk. The place smelled of antiseptic, which meant at least it was clean, and there were dog pictures hanging on the beige walls.

"Hello," Halley said.

"Hi!" Lyndie jumped up from her seat. "I'm so glad you're here early. We're going to have a lot of people show up to claim pets they looked at yesterday. It's empty now so Gail will have time for you."

"Yay for good timing," Halley said.

Lyndie grinned. "Why don't you fill out the paperwork first so that's complete. I'll give it to Gail and then she'll come talk to you." She picked up a clipboard with forms attached and handed it to Halley.

She sat down in a chair and filled out the detailed

questionnaire. Besides the basics, name and address, etc., it asked if she'd ever owned a dog, if she was home or worked during the day, how long the dog would be alone, and other things. They also asked for references, so she put down Kane and her sister, who she'd then texted and given a heads-up that she might be getting a call.

Halley answered the form honestly, hoping they wouldn't hold the fact that she'd never been a pet owner against her.

She handed back the clipboard and asked, "Can I see Monty?"

Lyndie smiled. "You bet. I'll go get him and Gail. Be right back." She walked out a door behind her and returned minutes later with the small black dog in her hands. "Here you go," she said, handing her the dog.

She snuggled him into her neck and inhaled his shelter smell, wrinkling her nose. "You need a bath," she whispered, knowing that would be her first order of business if she was lucky enough to be able to take him home.

About ten minutes passed, after which a tall redhead walked into the front of the shelter. Lyndie disappeared into the back room.

"Hi. You must be Halley. I'm Gail Spencer."

"It's nice to meet you," Halley said.

"I see you two are bonding?"

She nodded. "He's such a sweet boy."

"He is. He's come a long way. You'd be getting a real gem. He's housebroken and crate trained but he's also very much a Velcro dog. Meaning, he wants to be where his people are. I looked through your forms briefly and I see you work from home."

She nodded. "I paint. Of course, I'd keep all my supplies up high and away from him," she rushed to assure Gail.

"That's good to know and a plus for a dog like Monty. We've grown very attached to him, but I have a German shepherd who needs long walks and I've had to separate them sometimes. My shepherd girl is a bit territorial."

"I understand."

They spoke for a little longer, and all the while, Halley held Monty in her lap. The little dog snuggled against her stomach, a feeling of warmth and attachment filling her.

After a bit, Lyndie walked over and gave Gail a thumbs-up.

"Your references checked out and I like you," Gail said. "You've got yourself a dog."

Halley's breath left her in a rush and unexpected tears filled her eyes. "He's mine?"

"A little more paperwork, a payment, I'll give you a list of items you can buy, and come back for him whenever you're ready." Gail's smile thrilled Halley because she knew the woman wanted to give him to the right home and she approved of her.

Halley kissed Monty's smelly head. "I'm going to give you the best home, sweet boy. We're going to have a good life together."

"I'm sure you are," Gail murmured.

Halley spent the next few hours buying pet supplies, taking everything home, and setting up her house. She put a crate in her bedroom and another in the same room as her easel, just in case she needed to lock him up safely, dog bowls, food, toys... so many toys, and assorted other things on the list given to her by the shelter.

She returned later in the afternoon and took her dog home.

KANE HAD NEVER seen Halley so content as she'd been over the last week. Bringing Monty home had done something to soothe her soul. She'd needed the dog as much as he'd needed her, especially after Kane had forced her to relive that horrible night in her past. He ought to feel guilty about dredging up the memories, but he still believed she'd needed to exorcise them by talking. He hoped she'd stop dreaming about it someday.

Right now it was early morning and he was catching up on paperwork before heading to work on cars for the day, and he needed to focus more on the pages in front of him and not his personal life. He worked for another half hour, lost in thought when he was interrupted.

"Kane?" His sister came up to where he sat in the office of the garage.

"Hey, Andi. What's up?" He couldn't imagine why she was here instead of at work at the flower shop.

She settled into the chair across from the metal desk. "Dad's up. Or should I say not up. He's sleeping instead of getting up for work."

"Shit. I hadn't looked at the time. I'll call him."

"Don't bother. I woke him and he said to go away, so whatever. That's the least of my problems."

He narrowed his gaze. "What else is going on?"

She leaned forward and propped an arm on the desk. "I went to my wallet this morning to give Nicky money for a class trip, and I was short about a hundred dollars. I just went to the bank yesterday, so I know what I had in there."

Ugly reality settled on his shoulders. "You've got to be shitting me," he said, though he knew she wasn't. He ran a hand through his hair, wondering what their next step should be.

"I don't know if I can keep doing this," she said. "I

know I'm living in his house, but I'm paying for everything, which I don't mind, but I can't keep feeling like I have two children to worry about. I think Nicky and I need to move out."

Her words smacked him hard, but he understood where she was coming from. "How about we sit him down together and give him a choice. He can move into an apartment and pay for himself or you and Nicky can rent a place." Either way she wouldn't be living with the day-to-day problems of an addict.

She twisted a strand of her hair between her fingers. "That would work," she murmured, looking as sick as he felt at the prospect of confronting their father.

He reached out and grasped her hand. "It'll be okay. Either way. And if you need to move, I'll look with you and help you out. I bet there are some houses for rent that you can afford. I'd hate to see you move into a smaller apartment, coming from a house with a yard."

His nephew loved playing basketball on the driveway and riding his bike, and Kane didn't want to take that away from him because his grandfather was irresponsible and had an addiction problem.

"Thanks, Kane. I hate to make it your problem."

"Hey. He's our father. I think that makes it our problem. All the responsibility shouldn't fall on you."

"Okay." Her shoulders relaxed at his reassurance. "So what's going on with you and Halley?" she asked. "Is everything good?"

"I think so." He hoped so. He'd pushed her and she'd forced him to leave, but he hadn't gotten the sense she was upset with him.

And when he'd worked at her house this week, their routine had been normal. She cooked dinners, they hung out, occasionally had sex if he wasn't too exhausted from working and she was in an upbeat mood. He just couldn't shake the feeling that she wasn't as all in as he was and it bothered him. Or more likely, she wouldn't let herself fall hard because of those damned walls she had up. He wasn't sure what else to do to get her beyond her past and to be able to trust.

"I like her," Andi said, interrupting his thoughts. "When I stopped by to apologize for dad's behavior at dinner... well, for arguing in front of her, she was really great. We talked for a while. I think she's good for you. She's so understanding and sweet. Unlike an unmentionable woman in your past."

He frowned at her for bringing up Liza, but he was glad his sister liked Halley. It meant a lot to him that the two women in his life got along, more that they liked one another.

"I'll forgive you for mentioning the bitch," he muttered. He picked up a pen and rolled it between his hands, a gesture he always found soothing. "But yeah. Halley's great. She has her own issues that keep me at a distance sometimes." He wouldn't be sharing that information with his sister. It wasn't anyone's business but Halley's.

"I know there's been a lot of gossip about her and her family over the years, but she seems to have her head on straight regardless of what went on in her past." Andi wrinkled her nose. "Then again, perception can be just that. But if anyone can get through to her, you can."

He laughed. "Thanks for the vote of confidence."

"No problem." She picked up her purse and rose to her feet. "Okay, I'm late as it is. I need to get to work."

He walked her to the door. "Let's pick a time to talk to Dad."

"Yeah," she said on a sigh. "Maybe Sunday night?"

He nodded. "Works for me." There'd never be a good moment for that conversation, so they might as well just bite the bullet and dive in.

Chapter Eight

HALLEY WAITED AT the coffee shop in town for her mother to show up as planned. She sat outside with an iced cappuccino and a cinnamon roll, the sun shining, Monty on his leash, lying down beside her. Things were good, if she wasn't so wary about dealing with her mother.

Not that Meg had done anything to set off alarm bells, but that was the issue. After her aunt's dire warning, her mother was acting so genuine. Calling every few days, asking about her life, being present and there. It was confusing because of how much Halley wanted to believe prison time had changed her.

She glanced up as her mother approached, dressed better than the last time Halley had seen her, wearing a pair of white capris and a red top.

She smiled as she settled down into a chair. "I'm sorry I'm late. The bus was running behind schedule."

Halley smiled. "It's fine. It's a gorgeous day and

Monty loves being out and about." She leaned down and scratched the dog's head.

"Oh, look at him," her mother said. She picked him up and held him up for inspection.

Monty was now clean, fluffed, and so sweet.

"He's adorable. How old is he?"

"The vet thinks he's about three," Halley murmured. The same age as she'd been when she was sent to foster care. There was something both ironic and meant to be about it all, she thought, before turning back to her mother. "How are you?" she asked, not wanting her mind to dwell on the past while she sat across from the woman whose actions had led to it all.

Her mother put Monty back down and met Halley's gaze. "Not bad. I got a job at a convenience store within walking distance from where I live." She leaned back in her seat.

"That's wonderful." A first step, Halley thought. A big one, too. If her mother could pay her own way, that would go a long way toward proving herself to her sister and to Phoebe. Who Halley still hadn't told she'd been in touch with Meg.

Her mother frowned. "It pays the bills but not by much. And the hours are long and in the evenings. But I'm managing."

"Good. It won't be easy, I'm sure, but things will get better." Halley paused, then asked, "Would you like something to drink?"

Her mother nodded and gestured for the waitress. She ordered a large coffee, light with sugar, and turned back to Halley. "How's your painting going?"

"Very well, actually. I seem to have broken through a block and I love my newest work. Faith, the gallery owner, called this morning when I was walking Monty. We've been playing phone tag but I'm hoping for good news about a sale." At least, that's what Faith had alluded to in her earlier message.

Her mother placed a hand on top of hers. "I'm so proud of you."

At the motherly gesture, Halley's eyes filled with tears.

"I guess that brings me to what I should have said last time I was at your house." Her mother shifted uncomfortably in her seat.

"Which is?"

She leaned forward and said, "I'm so sorry. I'm sorry I wasn't the mother you deserved. I'm sorry I was so lost that you were taken away and I'm sorry for whatever you went through when you were in foster care."

Her words took Halley by surprise, but the conversation she'd had with Kane was still lingering on her mind, the subject too raw. "That's over," Halley said too sharply, immediately regretting her harsh tone.

Just then, the waitress returned with her mother's drink, and they both waited until they were alone.

Her mother spoke first. "I never, ever meant to get so into drugs that you girls suffered. I'll never forgive myself. I just hope you can forgive me one day."

Halley managed a smile though it wasn't easy. Still, her mother was reaching out and she seemed so sincere. "I'm trying," she said and meant it.

Everyone had the potential to make bad choices, she thought. Her mother's decisions had led to addiction, and things had spiraled out of control. But she'd paid her dues and she wasn't living an easy life now. Halley actually felt bad for her, knowing she was struggling.

The waitress returned with a check in her hand and placed it down on the table.

"Thank you," Halley said. Before she could reach for the paper, her mother grabbed it.

"I've got it," she said.

"Oh. Well, thank you." It wasn't a big check and Halley let it go.

Her mom reached for her purse, dug around inside, and winced.

"What's wrong?"

Her mother's cheeks flushed red. "I don't have my wallet. I just have bus fare," she said without meeting Halley's gaze.

"It's fine. I've got it," Halley rushed to assure her, sensing the cost was more of an issue than she'd let on. "It's happened to me before, too." She fudged the truth to alleviate her mother's embarrassment.

Her mother smiled. "I'll get it next time."

Halley nodded.

They rose to their feet. Her mom walked over and pulled her into a hug for the first time. Halley's arms sat uncertainly at her side, and then, though it didn't come easily, she hugged her mother back.

"Halley?"

She froze at the sound of her sister's voice, stepping back from her mother and meeting Phoebe's gaze. "Umm, hi," she whispered.

Phoebe, dressed for work in a cream suit, looked at them, her gaze darting from Halley to their mother. The first time Halley had seen Meg, she'd had a sense of déjà vu, but she'd known immediately who she was, even if it had taken time to wrap her brain around the fact. Now her sister stared open-mouthed, and Halley watched as she processed the same way.

"How could you?" Phoebe finally asked. "Did you conveniently forget she abandoned us? Left us to the state's care? Did you blank on what you went through?" she asked, her voice rising.

"Phoebe, stop." She grabbed her sister's hand.

Meg, meanwhile, stood there looking at her oldest

child. "Phoebe? I'm sorry," she said, stepping forward. "I just want to apologize."

"Right. Because that makes it all better. Because it undoes all the harm you did. Oh! Did she hit you up for money yet, Halley? Because it's only a matter of time."

"Phoebe, she's changed. She's working on things. She has a job and she's trying," Halley said, defending their mother and surprising herself in the process.

Phoebe's jaw dropped and her mouth hung open. When she'd composed herself, she glared at Halley. "Now you're defending her! Mark my words, Halley. She wants something from you. She's just buttering you up so you'll hand it over."

Halley straightened her shoulders. "You're wrong," she said because she desperately wanted to believe it.

Their mother stood in silence, her cheeks flaming. People around them were watching, listening. This was going to be great gossip for the town. The Ward sisters had made a scene with their ex-drug-addict mother.

"I should go," their mother said. "I'll talk to you," she said to Halley before giving Phoebe one last lingering glance and walking away.

Phoebe glared.

"Come on," Halley said. "I'm allowed to have hope that she's changed."

Phoebe's face softened. "I'm just worried you're

going to be hurt when she shows her true colors. And you've been hurt enough."

Halley sighed. "I love you for caring but maybe this is something I have to learn for myself. Or maybe I won't have to because she really has changed."

"And pigs fly," her sister muttered.

"Can we agree to disagree on this?" Halley asked.

"Yes. Fine." Phoebe crossed her arms over her chest and met her gaze with a serious one of her own. "But listen, when she fucks up—"

"If—"

She shook her head. "When she does, I'll be there for you without saying I told you so. Deal?"

Halley dropped her shoulders and sighed. "Deal."

Phoebe pulled her into a long hug.

✧   ✧   ✧

KANE WAS BENEATH a car in the garage when Jackson yelled for him. "Harmon! Phone call!"

Kane slid out from his prone position and wiped off his hands. He pushed himself up and headed for the office to take the call, which turned out to be a client wanting to discuss whether it was worth putting money into his old car. After debating the pros and cons, he hung up and started to head back to the bay when his cell buzzed in his pocket.

He pulled it out and glanced at the screen to find a

text from Halley. *Sold painting to NYC gallery owner!*

The fact that she bothered to text him about her good news was huge and he grinned. *Celebration is in order*, he texted back.

A few hours later, Kane walked up the front steps to Halley's instead of going around the back the way he usually did when he came to work. He'd stopped by Andi's place of work and left with a bouquet of flowers, so he strode up the walk and rang her doorbell, planning to surprise her and hopefully take her out for dinner instead of having her cook for them both.

Although he loved her meals and the fact that she didn't mind cooking for him, he wanted to go out with her in public. To expose her to more of the world, and he didn't want her to have a chance to say no over the phone or via text.

He rang the bell. It took a while for her to open the door, and when she did, she looked surprised to see him.

She held Monty in her arms. "Kane! Why didn't you come around to the deck?"

He pulled the flowers from behind his back and held them out for her.

Her expression softened as she took in the bouquet. "They're beautiful! Thank you," she said, accepting the wild flowers.

He'd opted for a more casual bunch instead of roses because they reminded him of her spirit. Harnessed but waiting to be set free.

"How's the little man?" he asked, petting the dog's head.

"He's great. So to what do I owe the pleasure of your company?" she asked.

"Well, I was hoping to convince you to let me take you to dinner."

She stepped back and eyed him, looking him over from head to toe. "And that explains the nice jeans and the button-down shirt. Looking good, Mr. Harmon. Very good."

Her expression told him she liked what she saw and he grinned. "So what do you say?" he asked. "Let me take you out to celebrate your sale."

She grinned at that. "I'm really not dressed to go out." She gestured to the oversized tee shirt she often wore to paint.

He shrugged. "I can wait while you shower or wash up. No problem." He wasn't looking to give her an out.

"If you're sure you don't mind waiting."

He shook his head. For her? He could wait a lifetime, a revelation that should have shocked him but didn't. His feelings for her were real and had been building from the beginning. Acknowledging them now felt right.

He followed her inside and she filled a vase with water and arranged the flowers he'd bought inside. Then she headed to the living room area and placed the bouquet on a shelf near her easel. Monty followed her everywhere she went, his little paws clicking on the tile.

"Okay, well, let me shower and I'll be out in a few minutes. I have to get the paint off my hands." She waved them in the air. "And you can watch Monty."

At his name, the pup let out a high-pitched woof.

Kane played fetch with Monty and one of his toys until Halley returned, freshly showered, wearing a pastel blue dress, halter style, that still managed to show off her cleavage. And her hair fell softly over her shoulders, giving her a feminine, flirty, ever beautiful look.

Damn. He let out a low whistle. She spun and grinned. "You like?"

"I love it." So did his cock, which was erect inside his pants.

"Let me put Monty in his crate and I'm ready to go," she said, unaware of his physical discomfort.

A few minutes later, she slid a pair of gold sandals on her feet, grabbed her purse, and was ready to leave.

A short drive in his Camaro and they arrived at the Blue Wall, where his sister was working. The restau-

rant was crowded with people as they approached the
hostess stand.

"Hello, you two," Andi said.

"Hey, sis."

"Hi, Andi. It's good to see you," Halley said.

She smiled. "Kane made a reservation, so your table is ready." She gathered two menus and said,
"Follow me." She led them to a table in the back of
the restaurant, not secluded, because there was no
such thing in the restaurant, but at least they had some
privacy.

Kane smiled at the people he recognized as they
walked to the booth. He waited for Halley to sit and
settled in across from her, the low lighting casting her
in a soft glow.

The waiter immediately came by and took their
drink order. He asked for a bottle of champagne
because he wanted to celebrate her good news.

He met her gaze and smiled. "So tell me more
about this sale."

Her eyes lit up at the topic. "A man from a large
Manhattan gallery purchased the painting from Faith,
and he told her that if it sold well in his gallery, he
would be in touch with me for more of my work."

"I'm thrilled for you. I know this has been a dream
of yours." She spent so much time on her own that
the outside recognition must feel good.

"It has. And thank you."

Just then, the waiter returned with the champagne. He opened the bottle and filled their glasses before leaving the bottle in an ice bucket beside the table.

"To your success," he said, raising the glass and touching it to hers.

She grinned. "I'll toast to that."

They talked about his week and the variety of customers who'd come into the store before the waiter returned to take their orders.

"How's your dad?" she asked when they were alone.

He groaned at the question, hating to subject her to more conversation about his family issues. "Andi's had it. She wants to move out, and we're going to tell him at Sunday night dinner." He heard the defeat in his tone but he couldn't help it.

Understanding lit her gaze. "You can't change him. You know that, right? It's not your fault he can't get his gambling under control."

"Knowing it and really feeling it are two different things. I know he's making his own decisions, but I can't help feeling like I'm failing him and my sister somehow."

She shook her head, reaching across the table and putting her hand on his, curling her fingers into his palm. "You're strong for all of them, but you can't do more than you're doing."

It meant the world to him that she was here to listen. "I appreciate your support. What about you? You said you were meeting your mother today. How did that go?" He'd wondered about her visit all day, curious about whether her mother had continued to be contrite and apologetic without hitting her up for money.

"I had a great meet with my mother except that we ran into Phoebe and she wasn't happy. She read me the riot act about how she hasn't changed and I'll be sorry I opened myself up to her. And I surprised myself by defending my mother." She winced and pinched the bridge of her nose as if she were getting a headache.

"Are you okay?"

"Yeah. I just... I hate being in the middle and I don't want Phoebe mad at me. She said she isn't, so I'm glad, but I just know she's wrong. My mother apologized. I mean really apologized for what happened to us as kids. She took responsibility."

"I'm glad. That's what matters, right? You do what you feel is best for you, and your sister will do the same for herself. At the end of the day, you're two separate people."

She laughed. "You make it sound so easy."

"Any easier than me not blaming myself for my

father's actions?"

She shook her head. "Touché. Very good point," she said with a grin.

"I have my moments," he said with a wink.

Her cheeks flushed pink at that wink and he liked knowing he affected her.

She picked up her glass and his gaze was drawn to an oval opal ring on her finger. "That's a beautiful ring," he murmured, the blues and pinks glittering in the dim lighting.

"Thank you. My aunt gave it to me. It used to be her grandmother's. Phoebe got a necklace that was hers. Apparently they were close and my great-grandmother was nothing like her daughter—who was way too judgmental in life."

She held up her hand and studied the ring. "I always loved the colors in the stone, and since my birthday is in October, it's my birthstone. Just like my mother's and great-grandmother's, according to my aunt."

He was glad she had something that belonged to a good person in her family.

"I only wear it on special occasions." She met his gaze. "And tonight is one of those, thanks to you."

Yes, he thought. It definitely was.

She smiled and glanced down at her menu.

They ordered their meals, he chose a steak and she

picked lobster, and they relaxed, ate, and enjoyed each other's company. The whole time he watched her, surprised at the change he'd seen in her from the first day he'd picked her up on the side of the road.

She was open in her conversation. She laughed more and it lit up her beautiful face. He hoped he had something to do with the change, but he wasn't arrogant enough to take complete responsibility. Oh, hell. Yes, he was.

"Can I get you anything else?" the waiter asked.

Kane glanced at Halley.

She shook her head. "I'm good."

"Just the check, please," he said to the other man.

Halley placed her napkin on the table. "Before we go, I'm going to stop by the ladies' room, so if you'll excuse me, I'll be right back."

"I'll be waiting." He watched her go, those long, lean legs a sight to behold.

Imagining them wrapped around his waist as he fucked her caused a definite issue, and he had to alter his focus if he wanted to be able to walk out of the restaurant without anyone noticing his bulging erection.

This woman and the things she did to him… What had started with a broken-down car had led to something real. At least for him, and when he looked into her eyes, he saw more than friendship when she gazed at him. More than sexual attraction, of which they shared plenty. It was that more that had him wanting to take her home and into bed.

He wanted to show her what he felt for her because he didn't think she was ready for the words. Words he'd never said out loud to any woman in his adult life. He was hoarding them, saving them for when the time was right. Because what had begun with an agreement to take things one day at a time had left him completely invested, and he wanted to let her know.

HALLEY FRESHENED UP in the restroom. She washed her hands and swept a fresh coat of gloss over her lips, realizing this was the first time she'd willingly gone out without reservation. Kane had asked and she'd said yes. Easy as that.

She was changing, letting her mother into her life… letting Kane in. As much as trusting made her nervous, she had to admit she felt lighter and freer without that constant shadow of worry sitting on her shoulder. Phoebe had said to expand her horizons, and somehow, without planning to, she'd done just that. Maybe her sister didn't approve of all the ways in which she was reaching out, but Kane was right. Halley had to live life for herself.

And right now she had a sexy man waiting to take her home and to bed. Life was good, and when was the last time she'd actually had a positive thought like that going through her head?

She dropped her gloss into her purse and rushed back out to Kane, stopping short when she walked out of the restroom and saw he wasn't alone at the table.

Liza had shoved herself into his side of the booth, her ample and probably fake cleavage exposed above the V neck of her tight dress. She swallowed back the bite of jealousy, reminding herself that Kane, who was leaning back and away from her touch, didn't want to be with her, despite the fact that she obviously wasn't taking no for an answer.

Halley hadn't done confrontation with mean girls since foster care. Even in high school, she'd ignored the jibes about her being unwanted and unloved and turned into herself rather than argue or fight back.

But this was Kane and he was *hers*, and the more Halley watched, the angrier she got. She strode over to the table and glared at Liza.

"Did you not see the second champagne glass? Or do you just not care that he's not interested in you?" she asked Liza point-blank.

She didn't see the point in beating around the bush when the other woman was the type to deliberately ignore signals.

"Oh, I'm sorry. Was that you he couldn't wait to get rid of?" Liza asked in a catty voice.

"Oh, for the love of God. Go away, Liza. He's mine."

She huffed and slid out of the booth. "I'll come back when she's not around," Liza muttered and strutted away, her ass swinging as she walked.

Halley rolled her eyes. "Is she dense or what?"

"I'm yours?" Kane asked, pushing himself out of the booth and standing beside her.

She blushed a healthy shade of red, she was sure because her face was on fire. "Can we go now?"

She pivoted but he grasped her hand and turned her back. "Not until I hear you say it to me."

"Kane—"

He cupped her face in his hand. "If it's true, it shouldn't be so difficult to say."

He leaned down, his face inches from hers, the scent of his aftershave making her weak. She wondered if the rest of the restaurant was watching, but she couldn't bring herself to look away from his handsome visage or to care if they'd become a spectacle. "You're mine," she whispered.

His face lit up with pleasure.

"Now can we go home?"

His eyes gleamed as he grasped her hand and led her out of the restaurant, into his car, and drove her home. Of course, there was no rush to the bedroom, not with Monty whining from the crate. Turned out the dog had made a nice mess.

Kane groaned.

"I'll clean it. Would you mind running him outside?" she asked.

"No problem. I can do the messy work."

She shook her head. "I've got it. Honestly."

He scowled but did as she asked, hooked Monty up to his leash and took him out the door.

She pulled the pan out of the bottom of the crate and headed to the kitchen, removing her watch and placing it on the windowsill where she always put any jewelry she happened to be wearing. Then she slid her ring off her finger and placed that in the center of the closed metal watchband. She rinsed the pan with soap and water, dried it, and put it back inside the crate just as Kane returned.

"Come on, little man. Back inside," Kane said to Monty.

One look at the big, strong man walking the tiny dog and her heart turned over inside her chest. His hair fell over his forehead and she itched to brush it back, to run her tongue along his strong jaw and kiss those full lips. He was well-built, muscular, and so sexy he took her breath away, yet with the tiny dog he was gentle.

"Come on, Monty. Crate," she said, a dog treat in her hand.

Kane unhooked the leash and Monty went running into his den, eager to get his reward. She locked him up with his soft blanket and favorite toy and stood to face Kane.

He held out his hand and she walked over, sliding her palm along his. He curled his fingers, lifted his arm, and pressed his lips to her hand. Her skin tingled where his mouth touched her flesh and her nipples hardened into tight peaks.

"I want to make love to you," he said in a gruff voice.

His words wrapped around her, both alluring and frightening at the same time. Love was a foreign emotion to her. She'd never had love, not as a child, and as a teen, she'd been too traumatized to accept it.

She didn't doubt he'd chosen his words intentionally, but *I want to fuck you* would have been easier to hear.

✧ ✧ ✧

ONCE THEIR CLOTHES were off, Kane set about showing Halley how he felt about her. She lay on her back, and under the dim light of the lamp on the nightstand, he worshipped her body. He kissed her lips, then trailed his mouth down her neck, past her collarbone, and over her chest. He nipped and licked his way, taking his time, arousing her with every sip and nibble of his mouth and teeth.

She writhed beneath his ministrations, arching her back, bringing her breasts and nipples within tempting tasting distance. He dipped his head lower and sucked a nipple into his mouth, swirling his tongue over the tightened bud and flicking and pulling it between his teeth.

"Oh, Kane." She slid her fingers into his hair and pulled at the longer strands, yanking them harder with each swipe of his tongue and nip.

The sensation went straight to his cock, as it pulsed with need, demanding to be allowed inside her wet pussy. But he had a goal, overwhelming both her senses and her heart, and so he kept on demonstrating his feelings without words.

Words he was certain she wasn't ready to hear. He'd seen her face when he'd told her he wanted to make love to her. The flash of panic before she'd shuttered her expression and willingly followed him to the bedroom. Overwhelming her with sensation that caused her to *feel* was his only hope of breaking through her final walls.

He moved to the other breast, giving it the same thorough, sensual treatment before licking his way over her stomach, moving lower, trailing his way down her undulating flesh. He slid his tongue from her navel down to her silken sex, damp and waiting for him to seductively torture it next. He smelled her arousal, and it made his already tortured body even harder.

He parted her sex with his fingers, holding her open so he could swipe his tongue up her center, landing on her clit. She bucked beneath him, and he pinned her thighs with both hands, keeping up the pressure as he lapped at her like a delicious treat. She arched up, grinding her sex into his mouth, and he worked her hard until she climbed, inching higher until her legs began to tremble and shake. Finally, she soared, coming apart beneath him, and damned if he didn't grind his dick into the mattress as she flew, coming as close to premature ejaculation as when he was a horny teen.

He wiped his mouth against her thigh and slid up her body, taking in her sated expression. Her eyes were heavy-lidded, and her soft lips were parted to draw in breath, with a hint of a satisfied smile lifting her mouth.

Watching her, he gently swept a stray strand of hair off her face. Her gaze focused intently on his as he braced one hand beside her head and grasped his dick in the other, positioning himself between her thighs.

"Ready, beautiful?"

She nodded and he slid into her waiting heat.

A groan escaped her throat, and her hands came to his ass, holding on tight as he began to move, causing her hands to slip off as he pulled out, then thrust back in deep. She grabbed his shoulders, bracing, expecting him to take her hard and fast.

She was about to be surprised. He held back, jaw clenched against the need to take his own relief as quickly as possible. Instead he slid out excruciatingly slowly, then took her again in an intense glide home, grinding himself against her clit before easing out once more.

She moaned, her body shaking, and she wrapped her legs around his waist, clutching him harder, grinding their bodies together. He felt her trembling as her soft walls milked his cock hard, her dampness clasping him in heat. He'd wanted feelings to erupt from this joining, and his were out in full force.

Making love to her was everything—it encompassed him body, heart, and soul. He could only hope she was experiencing the same melting emotions that were rushing through him right now.

HALLEY KNEW SHE was in trouble. So much trouble, as Kane did as he'd promised, making love to her, his rocking motions so gentle as he took her higher. And she went along for the ride, lost in his thoroughness.

Every time he slid out, he thrust back, grinding against her, and waves of arousal washed over her along with a tidal wave of emotion she was helpless against.

She gripped his shoulders as the first wave hit, digging her nails into his skin. "Kane!" She screamed out his name, holding back the more serious words that threatened to erupt, the love she felt for this amazing man caught in her throat as she came.

He held her tight as she rode out her orgasm, rocking into her over and over, milking every last spasm from her body before taking his own release. Afterwards, he collapsed on top of her until he caught his breath and she inhaled his musky, male scent, the sensuality of the moment and the emotions caught inside causing a lump to form in her throat.

What did she do with these overwhelming feelings she was so afraid to name, let alone speak out loud? How did she trust herself to love him freely, to believe that she wouldn't ever be hurt?

She didn't know, but she understood that she had to find a way if she wanted a future with Kane. She just didn't know if she was fearless enough to manage the feat.

Chapter Nine

K ANE SPENT THE weekend working on Halley's deck, and she spent the time avoiding him, as if afraid any intimate contact would lead to serious conversation. From long walks with Monty to a headache she couldn't shake, to the Saturday night she'd spent alone working, she'd managed to find more time alone than with him, and he'd been at her house.

He'd known his approach, the deliberately slow seduction, could have her running scared, so he fought back his frustration and gave her the time she needed to come to terms with her feelings. Feelings he knew damn well she had for him. He'd seen it in her eyes as he'd made love to her and as she came for him long and hard.

Tonight, he and his sister were confronting their dad with Andi's plans to move out. So much for a nice, relaxing weekend, he thought, disappointed but not giving up on her. Not ever.

That night, he arrived at Andi's house to find Nicky shooting hoops outside as usual. Kane stopped to play a game of H-O-R-S-E with him before heading inside to see what awaited him.

He met up with Andi in the kitchen, where she was taking a roast chicken out of the oven. Wild rice sat in a bowl on the counter alongside asparagus with parmigiana cheese.

"Smells good, sis. Need help with anything?"

She smiled. "Thank you and no. I'm good. All I need is your support during the conversation with Dad." She moved the chicken to the cutting board and began to slice it up.

"Where's Dad?" he asked.

"Washing up. You know, I looked at a few rentals online. I think that's the route I want to go. Nicky and I need to have our own space. It's time," she said as she wiped her hands on a dishtowel.

"Then that's the direction we'll take. Don't worry. Dad's an adult and it's time he started acting like one. We've both made it too easy for him to backslide. You by paying the bills here and me by keeping him on at work even when he doesn't show up." Kane shook his head. "He might own the property but the business is in my name."

She nodded, shooting him a grateful glance.

"Okay. Nicky knows I want to move. I told him he'd stay in the same school district, so he took it well, but he's worried about leaving his grandpa. Let's not bring it up until he goes back outside to play."

Kane placed a reassuring hand on her shoulder. "Sounds like a plan. Can I bring the food to the table?"

"Sure thing. Thanks."

Just then, their father came into the kitchen, way too chipper, which set Kane's nerves on edge.

"Dinner smells so good, Andrea. Want me to get Nicky inside?" Joe asked.

"Thanks, Dad."

A few minutes later, after Nicky had washed his hands, they were seated at the table. They ate a drama-free meal, Nicky talking about seeing his best friend over the weekend and Joe cracking jokes.

Finally, Andi sent Nicky back outside to play, and Kane knew the ball was in his court as far as bringing up the subject they needed to address.

"Hey, Dad, what's with the good mood?"

Joe shook his head and didn't meet Kane's gaze. "Nothing you want to hear, son."

Aah. So more gambling. "I take it you were out with Walter last night?"

Joe nodded. "Andi hired herself a babysitter so she doesn't need me home." He didn't sound bitter about it, probably because it gave him free nights out.

Another step toward leaving their father, Kane thought. "So Dad, we need to talk to you."

Joe whipped his head up. "Don't want to hear about my gambling problems. I can stop any time I want."

He just didn't want to even try, Kane thought.

"This isn't about whether or not you have a problem, Dad," Andi said. "It's about me. And Nicky and what I need."

Joe lifted his head at that, clearly relieved the onus was off him. Or so he thought. "What's going on?" he asked, concerned. Because gambling aside, Joe Harmon was a caring father.

Kane braced his arms on the table. "Dad, Andi's decided—"

"It's time I move out," she said, taking over the conversation. "I want to get my own place for me and Nicky."

Joe looked stunned. He opened and closed his mouth again, clearly in shock. "But we have a good thing here."

"*You* have a good thing, Dad," Kane said.

He pushed himself up from his chair. "What's that supposed to mean?"

"Just that Andi pays the bills and you use whatever money you earn—"

"Or take from me," she added.

"—to gamble. And it has to stop," Kane said quietly but firmly. "It's too much for Andi to worry about you because she lives here and has to deal with knowing too much firsthand. Or the stress of knowing you'll steal money from her wallet. It's not fair."

Joe's shoulders slumped down, and he eased himself back into his chair. "I just borrowed a few dollars," he muttered.

"Dad," Andi said, exasperated. "On top of everything else, I need to have my own space. I've loved living with you but it's time."

He hung his head in what Kane assumed was a combination of shame and understanding.

Kane rose, walked over, and placed a hand on his father's shoulder. "We think you need help, but it's got to come from you. We're through torturing ourselves for what we can't change. But we love you, Dad. And we're here if you need us."

Joe remained silent.

"Dad?" Andi asked hesitantly. "You're going to have to start paying the bills for this house and that means budgeting. I can't tell you what to do about the gambling, but it's not going to help you do what you need to around here after I'm gone."

Joe muttered something under his breath. "I'll make it work," he said afterwards.

Kane didn't know how and was sure there would be many challenges ahead. But if his sister was free of the burdens around here, he'd deal with the rest as it came.

✧   ✧   ✧

HALLEY RECOGNIZED THAT she was being a coward by not facing her feelings for Kane. Or rather by being afraid of them. She had looked them in the eye when they'd made love on Friday night, and it scared her to death. He was being patient so far, but she didn't know how much longer that understanding would last.

She didn't have time to think about it now because her mother sat across from her in the kitchen, drinking a cup of coffee, Monty at her feet, gnawing on his bone that was bigger than he was.

"And so the man tried to walk out of the store with coffee and bread shoved under his jacket." Her mother laughed, shaking her head. "The store owner caught him and called the police. It was a complete nightmare with the cops coming and everything."

Halley grinned, enjoying this lighter side of her parent.

"Well, I suppose he got what he deserved."

"We all do eventually," her mother murmured.

"Mom, stop beating yourself up over the past. That's what it is and you did your time."

She sighed. "I know. It's just hard. At minimum wage, it's tough to make ends meet. I'm handling it but…"

Halley had been thinking about this for a few days now. She knew life was difficult for her mother, and this was the first time her mom had even slightly mentioned her plight or complained. Unlike what her aunt had—and still—thought, her mother was here to build a relationship. Halley felt it in her bones.

So making the offer she planned felt right, too. "Mom, let me write you a check. Just to tide you over a bit."

Her mother looked horrified. "No. I couldn't take money from my own child!" Her cheeks turned pink. "Thank you, honey, but I couldn't."

Halley shook her head. "I insist." She rose and headed to get her purse from the bedroom. "I'll be right back."

When she returned, her mother was washing her hands at the kitchen sink. "I spilled coffee over the top of the rim," she said nervously. "I just feel so uncomfortable taking from you."

"Stop." Halley folded the check she'd written in half and handed it to her mom. "Consider it a loan if you feel bad." At her mother's salary, Halley didn't expect to be paid back nor did she want to be, but if it let her mom retain her pride, let her think she would.

"Thank you." Her mother pulled her into a grateful hug. "I don't know what I did to deserve you."

Halley's heart softened even more. "You're welcome."

"So I need to go because I have a late shift at the store."

Halley nodded. "Today's house cleaning day for me." She planned to get started when her mother left.

"A woman's work is never done." Her mom laughed, gathered her things, and took off.

Halley spent the rest of the day scrubbing the bathroom, dusting the house, and doing laundry, feeling upbeat about her mom. The next time they were together she was going to gather the courage to ask about her sister, Juliette. She swallowed hard and continued her cleaning.

While in the bedroom, she noticed that her jewelry case was open, which reminded her she'd left the watch and ring she'd worn to go out with Kane on the windowsill in the kitchen.

A piece of hair had fallen out of her ponytail, and she pushed it out of her face, tucking it behind her ear as she walked to the kitchen and headed over to the sink. The watch remained in the same place but the ring was gone.

Her heart skipped a beat, her mind racing for an explanation that wasn't the one immediately rushing through her mind. If Halley had put the ring back in the case and forgotten, she would have put the watch away, as well. And there was no way the ring could have fallen into the sink because she'd have heard the sound since it was a substantial piece of jewelry. She bit down on her lower lip and paced the room, still fighting the inevitable conclusion.

Instead of panicking, she picked up the phone and dialed her mother, but there was no answer. The call went straight to voice mail.

No. Her mother had genuinely fought her on taking the check. One for five thousand dollars, Halley thought, her agitation growing. She'd wanted her mother to have some breathing room. And her mother had known Halley had left the kitchen in order to write the check, so her mother had no reason to take the ring. Except the ring had been there, in the circle of the watch.

Why not take the watch, too? Because her mother had probably figured out the obvious, that the timepiece wasn't worth money. It was a piece of junk, one with a nice look, but you could tell it was a fake. Halley bought it in a souvenir shop in town in case she forgot to take it off and accidentally wore it while painting.

But the ring? The ring was a family heirloom of sorts. It would have gone to her mother had she not been disowned, because October was her birthday, too, and the opal birthstone was unlucky, something that came from an old book in the 1800s. But she and her aunt had laughed about how fortunate Halley was to be able to own the gorgeous and expensive stone. She only took it out for special occasions, like her celebratory night with Kane. And now it was gone.

Her mother couldn't have known she had the ring, but she could have planned on taking something of value. Or she could have gotten lucky and seen the ring on the windowsill and she couldn't walk away from temptation. Did it really matter what her reason was?

She could have left the valuable piece of jewelry alone.

She could have valued her relationship with Halley, her daughter, above money, especially since Halley had gone to write her a check, anyway. The ring had just been a bonus. A windfall, really, since it was worth a small fortune.

Had this been her plan all along? Cozy up to Halley, pretend remorse, guilt, pain, soften her up so Halley would offer her money, which she'd done? Or had she just been waiting for an opening to steal something and run? She probably didn't even have a shift tonight. In all likelihood, she'd needed to make her escape before Halley looked at the counter and realized the ring was missing.

Her heart was racing inside her chest, her mother's betrayal pushing at her, mocking her for being such a fool. God, when would she catch a break? Her mother's neglect and drug use landed her in foster care, most of the homes had traumatized her in one way or another, then her mother returned and Halley was pathetic enough to open her heart only to have her mother stomp all over it.

When her phone rang, startling her, she jumped and grabbed her cell from the kitchen table.

"Hi, sis."

"Phoebe," Halley said dully, unable to even muster a faked normal tone. Nausea rose in her throat at the thought of telling her sister. Phoebe was going to kill her, not for the ring but for giving her mother a check. For believing in her. For being a gullible, naïve idiot who couldn't trust her own instincts on the one thing about which she should have known better.

"What's wrong?" her sister immediately asked.

"I... I... Something happened," Halley said, dropping to the nearest chair. Phoebe might say I told you so, but she'd also promised to be there for her, and Halley didn't have the strength to lie about what had happened.

"I'll be right there. Sit tight."

But she didn't. She couldn't just wait, because the nausea that threatened bubbled over, and she ran to the bathroom and threw up what little she had in her stomach. She dry heaved afterwards, physically and emotionally spent.

This, this had been the last straw. She was devastated over her mother's betrayal. This was the very reason she didn't open herself up to people—because they inevitably destroyed what little faith she had inside her. She was sad, tired, and heartsick over it all.

Half an hour later, Halley was crying in her sister's arms. She'd already soaked Monty's fur, the little dog licking her tears.

She'd tried to dial her mother a few more times only to get voice mail. She really had been played.

"I wanted to believe in her so badly I ignored the two people I should have trusted." Halley wiped at her eyes with her hands. "You and Aunt Joy warned me. I just thought—"

What? That she could wipe out the past by having her mother in her life in the present? Ridiculous, she realized now. She'd been blinded by hope and need and taken in by a woman who would always be a con artist.

Her sister grabbed a tissue from the box Halley had put on the kitchen table and handed it to Halley, then she smoothed Halley's hair off her face.

"You can put a stop on the check first thing in the morning," her sister said, and Halley nodded. She'd do that. It wouldn't change the emotions behind it, but it was something.

"Do you know what I love most about you?" Phoebe asked.

"What?"

"Your heart."

Halley opened her eyes wider. "Are you kidding me? I've done my best to keep the world out. What heart?"

"The bruised one in here." Phoebe tapped at Halley's chest. "You keep it hidden but it's there. You tell me you love me every time I see you. You want to make up for lost time. So as mad as I am at you for giving her a chance and worse for writing her a check, I understand why you did it."

Halley sniffed and blew her nose into the tissue. "Screw my heart," she muttered. It was as broken and damaged as the rest of her. Her mother had destroyed what was left along with any chance of finding Juliette, something she wouldn't bring up to Phoebe now. She would hold that knowledge inside. Phoebe never thought they had a chance with their mother anyway.

Phoebe shot her a sad look. "This awful feeling will pass."

"Doubtful." She vowed she wasn't going to allow herself to feel this kind of pain ever again.

"What about Kane?" her sister asked.

On hearing his name, her heart skipped a beat. "What about him?"

Phoebe shot her a knowing look. "Don't play dumb with me, Halley. You know what I'm asking."

She rubbed at her gritty eyes. "I'm going to tell him what happened and explain why we're over."

"No! You can't end things with him!" Phoebe practically shouted at her. "You care about him."

She loved him but it wasn't enough. The emotion she'd been fighting all weekend flooded her now, when her defenses were down. Not just down, at their lowest. She loved Kane Harmon, but they couldn't possibly be together, because he deserved someone whole, someone who was emotionally available.

He deserved someone who wasn't afraid, and right now that's what Halley was. Afraid to live, to feel, to give of herself.

"I can't keep things going with him," she insisted. No matter how much it hurt to think about being without him, she couldn't leave things as they were, because as much as she feared getting hurt, she was afraid of hurting Kane even more when he realized that she wasn't capable of giving all of herself to him.

He'd said he loved her with his body, and she hadn't been able to reciprocate the emotion, fear taking hold, and that was before she'd had her heart sliced out by her mother.

Phoebe looked at her with sad eyes but Halley couldn't budge. "Kane needs someone who can give their whole heart and I'm not that woman." She shook her head, knowing the safest, smartest thing to do was to return to her way of life before Kane, in her safe little bubble where she didn't deal with people, and that way she couldn't be hurt.

She'd gone into the relationship broken, and nothing that had happened could change the fact that her childhood had rendered her incapable of giving a wonderful man like Kane everything in life that he deserved.

✧   ✧   ✧

KANE HAD HAD a shitty morning, coming off a shitty weekend. Monday dawned and his dad was banging around the shop, pissing everyone off with his bad mood and foul language. Kane had finally banished Joe to the garage to clean up in order to keep him away from customers and human beings in general.

He obviously wasn't dealing very well with Andi's proclamation that she was moving out. It'd probably hit him just how much a dent this new situation was going to put in his gambling money.

On top of that, Halley had gone MIA since midday yesterday when he'd left her house. He could have gone over, called, or texted her, but he'd had the distinct sense she'd needed time. Clearly his effort to push her into facing her emotions had backfired.

He'd given her last night, but he wasn't going to give her more than that. After work today, they were having it out. One way or another she was going to face him and deal with her feelings. Too bad he didn't know where they'd be when things shook out.

He walked into the garage only to find Liza there waiting for him. "Son of a bitch," he muttered. Could this day get any worse?

"What can I do for you?" he asked her.

"My low tire pressure light is on," she said, gesturing to her Porsche parked outside the garage.

"And a gas station could fix that in five minutes." He wiped his hands on a cloth he had hanging from his pocket.

"Come on, Kane," she purred, coming up to him and wrapping her arms around his neck. "We were good together. I know what you like in bed, and we can have a long month of fun before the summer ends." The scent of her perfume made him want to gag, and he grabbed her arms from behind his head.

Instead of taking the hint, she pushed him back to the wall and put her lips on his. Breaking her hold and her lip lock wasn't easy, not without hurting her, and he couldn't believe he was in this position with the woman.

"Oh, my God." Halley's voice whipped through him.

He shoved hard, sending Liza reeling back on her high heels, twisting her ankle as she stumbled. "Ouch!" she cried.

"Fuck." He reached out and grasped Liza's elbow to keep her from going down completely.

Halley looked at him with wide eyes and an utterly betrayed expression. No matter that she'd brushed off Liza's play at the restaurant the other night, this looked so much worse.

Halley spun around, clearly intending to go.

"Halley, wait."

"Kane," Liza wailed, but he ignored her. She'd done enough to fuck up his life in the last five minutes. He wasn't giving her another second of his time.

Halley didn't turn and strode out the door, so Kane brushed past Liza and ran after her. "Halley! It wasn't what it looked like," he said, well aware of how lame the words sounded.

She turned back. "It doesn't matter."

"The hell it doesn't. *We* matter."

She shook her head. "That's what I came to tell you. We're over."

"What?"

Sadness reflected back to him from her blue eyes.

"I can't do this and it's not about Liza."

He was certain her seeing him looking like he was kissing another woman hadn't helped, but something else was clearly wrong. "Talk to me," he said, as Liza strode out of the office and headed for her car.

Halley shook her head. "Just know it's for the best."

She pivoted back and walked to her car. Sensing he'd get nowhere if he pushed her now, not after what she'd just seen, he backed off.

But that didn't mean he was going down without a fight.

✧   ✧   ✧

THAT NIGHT, HALLEY walked down to the beach and stuck her toes into the lapping water. She left Monty in the house because she didn't want to lose sight of him in the dark or worry about him even on a leash. She wrapped her hands around her knees and watched the waves crashing over the sand, but she didn't find the peace the scenery normally gave her.

Her stomach churned harder than the water rising up and then receding. How had her life gotten so out of control in such a short time? First, her mother, who still wasn't answering calls. If they hadn't fallen into a pattern of her mother calling often or getting back to her quickly, Halley would have given her the benefit of the doubt.

But this felt like a complete ghosting. Meg had gotten what she'd needed from Halley and now she was gone. Until next time, when she needed something. Who knew what she'd do then. The only thing Halley was certain of was that she'd never let herself be open or gullible again.

Then there was Kane. She'd gone over to talk to him. To explain what had happened with her mother and let him off the hook because he deserved someone stronger, smarter, better in his life. And she'd seen Liza wrapped around him like a leech.

She swiped at her eyes, wondering how had he gotten into a position where he was *kissing* Liza. Her stomach cramped at the painful memory. Halley didn't think he'd initiated the kiss, nor did she believe he desired it. Deep down, she knew there was an explanation that revolved around that bitch pushing herself on Kane, but as she'd told him, it didn't change things.

Halley knew she wasn't easy to be with. A relationship with her wasn't simple or laid-back. She was a loner for a reason, and she was so sick of reiterating to herself all the reasons he deserved someone unafraid of living. He just did, and for that reason, she'd had to let him go.

Chapter Ten

FUCK, FUCK, FUCK. How the hell had things with Halley gotten so screwed up? Kane ran a hand through his hair and groaned. His head was still spinning. From Friday night to tonight, things had gone sideways.

He'd called and texted Halley but she wasn't replying. He could go over there but he wanted to respect her space for now. Giving her time to accept that Liza had all but attacked him seemed smart. After all, he'd explained himself in nauseating detail via text and messages. If she'd wanted to talk to him, she'd get in touch.

Her silence was killing him.

As the days passed, he wanted to throttle Liza more and more because that kiss hadn't helped his cause. If Halley had come to break up with him, without that clinch, he might have made a strong appeal to her emotions. Instead she'd frozen him out.

And the fact that she'd come to end things regardless confused him. What had happened to make her want to call things off?

Knowing he needed answers and understanding they wouldn't come from Halley, he drove to the Ward estate on the outskirts of town, intending to talk to her sister.

He pulled past two large pillars with a plaque on which the family name was engraved and past the main house to the guesthouse on the far side of the estate. He knew from Halley that her sister lived there, and since it was late in the evening, he hoped to catch up with her there.

He knocked on the door and Phoebe answered immediately. "Kane!" She stepped aside so he could enter.

The sisters looked so different it always surprised him, Phoebe with her white-blonde hair and Halley with her brown. Their features weren't similar, either, but they clearly had a bond, which was the reason he was here.

"I wish I could say this was a surprise." Phoebe frowned. "This is about my sister, isn't it?"

He nodded and stepped into the house.

"Come, we can talk in the living room."

He followed her past the entryway and into the house, turning when they reached a room with two floral couches where they could sit.

He settled in across from Phoebe.

"So I'll break the ice," she said. "I heard what happened yesterday."

He winced. "Yeah. Well, it wasn't pretty. It also wasn't what it looked like, no matter how bad it appeared." He knew he was justifying, but it was the truth.

"I know. And I think deep down Halley does, too."

He ran a hand through his hair. "The thing is, she was coming over to end things anyway… and I want to know why. No, I *need* to know why. Because I can't fix what I don't understand."

Phoebe crossed her legs and leaned back in her seat. "Normally I'd say it was Halley's story to tell, but in this case we both know she won't do it. So I agree with you. You need to know."

She twisted her hands in front of her while Kane waited.

"It's about our mother."

His shoulders tensed at that. "You're fucking kidding me."

She shook her head. "My too naïve sister felt bad for her and gave her a check for five thousand dollars. While she was in the other room writing it out, our mother stole a family ring that Halley had left on the windowsill above the sink."

He winced and let out a groan. That ring had meant so much to her. Kane wasn't sure what shocked him less. That Halley had reached into her pocketbook to help the woman she desperately wanted a relationship with or the fact that her mother had stabbed her in the back.

"Damn," he muttered.

"To add insult to injury, our mother has dropped off the face of the earth. From constant talking and returning calls, Mother has disappeared on Halley. Completely."

He wiped his hands across his face, rubbing his eyes with both palms. "So she feels betrayed."

"Pretty much. She stopped payment on the check, so that's something. But she's devastated, and it's our mother's fault for fracturing the strength Halley was starting to build. Now she thinks you deserve someone stronger than her, someone who isn't afraid to live. She just wants to go back to the way she was and curl into a little self-protective ball, paint, eat, and barely live."

His stomach churned at the thought. "How she was when we met."

Phoebe nodded. "Exactly."

"I have to get her past what happened with Liza, first."

She shook her head. "No, you don't. Halley's a lot of things but she isn't stupid. She knows you and she told me about the woman's behavior at the Blue Wall. Like I said, deep down she doesn't blame you."

He hoped to God that was true.

"This is all about getting her past her fears and believing she can give you everything she thinks you deserve in life," Phoebe said. "Remember, the only two people she's stepped out of her shell for were our mother… and you. Our mother's a lost cause, but in her heart, she knows you aren't. She just has to believe in herself again."

"I'll do whatever I can to bring her out of this," he swore.

Phoebe shook her head. "Frankly these are Halley's issues, not yours. I'm not certain there's anything either one of us can do to get her past it. It has to come from her."

Kane nodded, pain slicing through him as he realized Phoebe was right. He couldn't change Halley's fears and insecurities. Only she could tackle those things. Which meant all he could do was settle in and wait.

HALLEY WALKED DOWN the aisle of the grocery store, filling up the cart with necessities for her meals. Her fridge was empty and she needed food to survive. These days, she wasn't doing much else beyond living, breathing, eating, and painting.

But her painting sucked. Nothing came out right. The colors were bland, the expression nonexistent. All the gains she'd made this summer were gone.

If the New York City gallery owner called with interest, she'd have nothing to give him, because her paintings matched her mood. Her life. Sure, she had things stocked up from the short time she'd painted with freedom in her heart, and she could give those, but what she was doing now was different. Stale, she thought and sighed.

She turned her cart into the produce aisle and nearly hit a shopping cart with her own. "Sorry!" she said and glanced up and into Joe Harmon's gaze.

"Hi, Mr. Harmon."

"Halley, good to see you."

"You, too." Except it didn't help her mood that he looked so much like Kane, from his facial features to the color of his hair, albeit his had a sprinkling of gray.

God, she missed Kane.

"How are you?" she asked when he didn't move on with his cart.

"Sucky," he muttered, and she tried not to chuckle at his grumpy word choice. "Andi's moving out. And she says I have to start doing things for myself so she knows I'll be okay on my own. So here I am, buying healthy food," he muttered.

Halley bit the inside of her cheek. She'd known Kane and Andi were having this talk with their father, but she hadn't had a chance to find out how things went. And she'd been too wrapped up in her issues with her mother to think about Kane's situation.

Embarrassment and shame filled her at the thought. He'd probably needed someone to talk to and she hadn't been there. More proof he needed someone less self-absorbed, someone more giving than she could be.

"He's miserable, you know," Joe said, taking Halley off guard. "And if you think two unhappy Harmon men make for a good working situation, you're dead wrong."

Her eyes filled with tears. "I'm sorry for that, Joe, but I'm just not ready for a relationship." Her greatest fear was that she never would be. That she'd never be able to trust her instincts enough to open her heart to love someone, and be loved in return.

"He told me about that Liza woman. She attacked him, you know. Grabbed him hard and sealed her lips over his. He couldn't extricate himself without doing her harm. And my son's a decent man."

Halley swallowed hard. "I know," she whispered. And she'd pretty much come to the same conclusions about the situation herself. It wasn't Kane holding her back, it was herself.

"I loved my wife," he said in reply.

She didn't understand the subject change. "I'm sure you did," she murmured.

He inclined his head, studying her.

She gripped the cart tighter in her hand.

"I gambled while she was alive. It's just that she made it better for the kids. I wasn't perfect but I loved her and she loved me back despite my failings. Whatever failings you think he has, they can't come near mine. And if my wife could love me despite it all, why can't you do the same for him?"

God. The poor man thought the kiss was the reason for the breakup. Because she hadn't told Kane why she'd come to end things. So he was clueless, too. Why hadn't she realized that before now?

Selfish, she thought. Wrapped up in her own head, the way she'd been her whole life.

"Promise me you'll think about what I said?" Joe asked.

"I promise," she murmured.

They parted ways and she was shaking, confused about what to do. She wanted Kane more than she'd ever believed possible. She just didn't know how to get past her fears.

✧   ✧   ✧

A FEW WEEKS passed, weeks during which Halley returned to her normal life except for the fact that she had a show at a New York City gallery to plan for. While she was excited, realizing her dreams were coming true, she felt empty inside. It didn't help that she'd had to choose paintings to send to the gallery, and though she had a few special ones she hadn't already given to the place in town, the bulk of her stored work came from the ones painted before the summer—before Kane had entered her life and opened up her world—and the ones she'd done recently, after she'd deliberately closed herself off again.

The show was a mixed blessing. She'd hoped a gallery would pick up her work and not want the artist to attend an opening event, but that wish had been futile, and deep down she'd known better. So she'd spent most of August talking herself into believing that she could handle the attention and the people, that stepping out of her comfort zone for this one thing was the right move. It was the only way to advance her career and keep her self-supporting and since she didn't want to live on family money, she was going to do the show. Somehow.

For the first week after they'd broken up, Kane had tried to text and call, but she'd decided cold turkey was the way to go, and after a while, he'd gotten the hint. He'd stopped trying to contact her, and he hadn't come to fix her deck, either. What did she expect when she'd pushed him out of her life?

Monty had become her comfort. If she'd thought an emotional support animal was a good idea when Kane was in her life, it was an even better one now.

✧   ✧   ✧

KANE KICKED AROUND the office, alternately yelling at his father for getting under foot and griping at Jackson for not finishing cars on time even though they were ahead of schedule. He was in a piss-poor mood and had been for weeks. He'd have thought he'd get past it by now, the longing and the missing Halley, but the more time that passed, the worse he felt.

Jackson thought he should pick up someone at the Blue Wall tonight, but the thought of being with any other woman turned his stomach. He tried to refocus on the receipts in front of him, but he couldn't concentrate, so when he heard the sound of heels clicking, indicating a woman was walking into the office, he looked up, eager for the distraction.

The woman with the pale blonde hair and business suit took him by surprise. "Phoebe," he said, covering his shock. "Something wrong with your SUV?" He grasped onto the most mundane reason for her to be here.

Why jump to Halley when she wanted nothing to do with him?

Phoebe shook her head. "I shouldn't be here but I thought you would want to know."

Worry suddenly filled him. "Is Halley okay?"

"If miserable is fine, then yes. She's just great," she said sarcastically.

He supposed it should make him feel better to know she was as unhappy without him as he was without her, but it didn't. He wanted her to have the life she desired, not be sad.

"So what can I do for you then?" he asked, rubbing a pen between his palms.

"Halley has a gallery opening in Manhattan Friday night. Her paintings are being shown and... well... I thought you'd want to know."

Wow. Her dreams were coming true. He wasn't surprised. She really was talented, and he was thrilled someone in the position to know and help her succeed had recognized that fact. "I'm happy for her."

Phoebe nodded. "Me, too. Here's the gallery information in case you want to take a trip."

He glanced at the card. The city was an hour or so from Rosewood. If he wanted to go, he could easily drive in and return home. To support her, nothing else.

He had no expectations where Halley was concerned. Enough time had passed that he realized if she missed him and wanted to get in touch, she would have.

"Thanks for letting me know," he said, uncertain of what he'd decide to do.

If showing up to support her was the right move, he'd do it in a heartbeat, but if he'd just upset her with his presence, he didn't want to ruin her big night.

"I think it would mean a lot to her if you showed up," Phoebe said as if reading his mind. "You know, so she isn't so alone. You know how uneasy strangers and crowds make her feel."

He nodded. He knew. Which meant if she was stepping out of her comfort zone to do this event, it meant a lot to her. More than he did, since she was unwilling to take that leap of faith for him.

"Just think about it," Phoebe said.

"I will. I'm just not making any promises."

Phoebe nodded in understanding. "Bye, Kane."

"Bye, Phoebe."

THE TIME FOR her show arrived, and though Halley had her sister and her aunt to accompany her to the city, she was a bundle of nerves.

Phoebe came over a few hours before they had to

leave to help her pick out a dress, and they'd been at it for the last thirty minutes.

"Go bold and bright," her sister said.

Halley pinned her with an *are you serious* stare. "This from the woman who wears white, winter white, beige, and cream as staples in her wardrobe." She raised an eyebrow at her sister.

"I'm not the star of the show."

"Don't say that." Just thinking about it made Halley want to puke.

"Okay, what about this?" Phoebe pulled out the pretty blue chambray halter dress she'd worn when Kane took her out to celebrate her first big sale.

Although the sight of it made her sad, it also made her feel closer to Kane, and she agreed, pulling the dress against her chest.

"You're not wearing those flat sandals you love, either. I brought you two pair of heels to pick from." Phoebe gestured to the shopping bag in the corner of her bedroom. "This is Manhattan we're talking about. You need to step up your game."

Halley sighed. "Okay. Heels it is."

"What about makeup? Want me to help?"

She rolled her eyes. "I'm not completely incapable of putting myself together," she muttered.

"No, you're not. But can I curl your hair?" Phoebe asked hopefully.

Halley laughed. "Yes, that you can do." They'd missed out on sisterly things like that growing up, and she was thrilled Phoebe wanted to do it now.

"Aunt Joy said she'd pick us up and drive us to the city." It was an hour's trip away, and Halley was grateful her aunt didn't mind weaving in and out of Manhattan traffic. It wasn't something she wanted to do herself.

They changed and dressed together, and Phoebe put some soft curls in her hair. She went a little heavier on her makeup than she normally would even for a night out and chose a nude pump from the two pair of heels her sister had brought over.

Before she knew it, she was standing at her own exhibition in New York City, her paintings on the walls and a glass of champagne in her hand, trying not to have a panic attack while she spoke to the owner.

Marc Renault, a good-looking man in his late thirties, with salt-and-pepper hair, was introducing her to someone interested in, surprisingly, one of her older paintings.

She caught her sister's eye. Phoebe gave her a thumbs-up, and Halley took a deep breath and managed the conversation with them both with a smile on her face.

She turned to give Phoebe a return thumbs-up when she caught sight of Kane standing beside her sister, Andi along with him.

Shock rippled through her at the familiar sight of him in dark jeans and a black tee shirt, fitted tightly over his well-defined muscles. He looked out of place among the men in suits and ties, and oh so welcome to her. How had he known to come tonight?

A glimpse at her sister's guilty face and Halley knew. She ought to strangle her sister for arranging for Kane to be here. As much as she wanted to see him, it hurt so much to meet his gaze and know he was no longer hers.

You made the choice, she told herself. *He's better off, and in the long run, so are you.* Except when he started toward her, she had a hard time believing anything she told herself for preservation.

"Hi," he said, coming up beside her.

"Hi," she murmured. "Thank you for coming."

"I wouldn't miss your first show. I know how much tonight means to you." He met her gaze, his dark brown eyes lingering on her face.

He was so sweet and such a good man. "Thank you. How have you been?" she forced herself to ask, hating the awkward pleasantries between them.

"Doing well." He was lying. He had the same dark circles under his eyes that she'd had to cover with makeup under hers. "You?" he asked.

"I'm… good." She choked the words out. "Getting this show was incredible." So why didn't she feel as happy as she ought to?

"I'm glad. If this makes you happy…" He waved an arm around the gallery. "Then this is what you need to do." He leaned in, his warm, familiar scent beckoning to her, and kissed her on the cheek. "Good luck," he whispered before turning and walking away.

At the sight of his retreating back and the ghost of his lips on her skin, her throat clogged with tears. His words echoed in her mind. *If this is what makes you happy, then this is what you need to do.*

But she wasn't happy. Not without him. Everything that had given her satisfaction before Kane was empty without him in her life, including her salvation, her painting.

All her reasons for pushing him out of her life, all the things she believed he deserved, that she hadn't thought she could give him… that was all she wanted to do now.

And the tears pouring down her cheeks told her that her excuses had been just that—a lie to cover her own fears. Well, what did she have in her life now besides those fears? Not a damned thing.

Because she didn't have Kane.

It had taken painful time apart and seeing him show up for her tonight to make her realize what a fool she'd been. She'd been so destroyed by her mother's betrayal, she'd crawled back into her shell and pushed away the one person who had shown her life, love, and true happiness. She needed to fix things if that was at all possible.

The next few hours of the exhibit were the longest of her life. She was contractually obligated to be here, and so she stayed until the bitter end, all the while second-guessing herself and her choices.

And if she thought the show was long, the ride back to Rosewood was interminably longer. Phoebe and her aunt chatted about her success and how proud they were of her—and Halley appreciated it, she did, but all she wanted was to get back home, change out of these uncomfortable heels, get in her car, and drive over to Kane's.

She didn't know what awaited her when she got there, whether or not he'd welcome her or turn her away. She'd hurt him badly and didn't deserve a second chance. But she desperately wanted one, and she would do whatever she had to in order to convince him she was sorry. She understood now how much she'd lost and desperately wanted him back.

For the first time in her life, she wanted to be brave. She wanted to be fearless. For herself, and for Kane.

✧　✧　✧

KANE DROPPED ANDI off at her house. She'd taken the night off from work to go with him to the gallery opening, and he was grateful. Their father, who, after his initial grouchiness, had been on his best behavior, had volunteered to watch Nicky while they were gone. Now Kane was back home and more tortured than ever.

Seeing Halley, in the same blue dress she'd worn the night he'd taken her to celebrate her first big painting sale to a New York City gallery, had been a punch in the gut. She'd looked beautiful, with her hair falling in soft curls around her face, but she'd also appeared fragile.

He knew the stress of a public showing had to have taken its toll on her. Had her sister been there leading up to the event to hold her hand? To reassure her she could handle it? He hoped so. Still, despite her fears, she'd accomplished her huge goal, and for that he was damn proud of her.

It'd been a long drive to and from the city and bed was calling him. He pulled off his shirt and was about to shed his jeans, as well, when a knock sounded at his door.

He assumed it was his father. Who else would visit at this late hour? He pulled the door open.

"Halley." He breathed out her name, shock rippling through him at the sight of her.

She still wore the blue dress, though she'd changed out of the heels that were so unlike her he'd assumed they were Phoebe's doing. And she'd pulled her hair into a ponytail, which meant she looked more like *his* Halley than she had earlier tonight.

"Hi. Can I come in? I'd like to talk."

He nodded and stepped aside for her to pass before shutting the door behind her. He inhaled the sweet scent of her shampoo and his cock hardened behind his jeans. Damn. Would he ever not react to being near her? Would there ever be a time when he didn't want her?

"I've never been to your apartment before. Can you believe that?"

Yes, he thought, because they'd spent all their time at her house. "This is home."

He gestured to the den-like area where he hung out. He had a television on the far wall and a couch across from that. A small table and two chairs made up the eating area, and the kitchen was to the right of the entry. To the far back was his bedroom and bathroom. That was it.

"It's small but cozy," she said, stepping in to the center of the room. "Can we sit?"

He nodded.

Fuck, this was awkward. Nothing between them had ever been uncomfortable before now, not even in the very beginning, when she was pushing him away. His heart hurt at the knowledge they were so far apart.

"What can I do for you?" he asked. Might as well get to the point of the visit. Before his whole damned apartment smelled like her long after she was gone.

She glanced down at her hands, which she was twisting together in her lap. "I appreciate you coming tonight. You'll never know how much your support meant to me especially since we're... you know."

"Broken up?" He wasn't going to cushion his words for her delicate sensibilities. She'd caused this. She could face it.

She nodded and cleared her throat. "Here's the thing. When I ended things, I thought I had a good reason. I'd just gone through some major trauma with my mother, and I didn't want to deal with life. With anyone. I was afraid. And you... you're so alive, Kane. You vibrate with life and you aren't afraid to live it."

"Look, I know about your mother, the check and the ring. Phoebe filled me in when you wouldn't."

She nodded. "I'm sorry I didn't tell you myself."

"I don't want your apologies. I really don't."

"Okay," she whispered. "It's just that at the time I thought you deserved so much more than I could ever give you. I wasn't willing to open myself up emotionally the way I would have needed to in a relationship."

"And don't you think it was up to me to decide

what I *deserved* or wanted from you?"

She ducked her head, then straightened her shoulders and met his gaze, like she'd just had a lecture with herself and decided to face him, after all. "Maybe but I knew you would wait for me and I didn't want that. I didn't want enough for myself and I wanted much more for you."

His hands hung between his knees as he studied her. "I appreciate the explanation."

She swallowed hard. "That's not all. When you showed up tonight, when you told me if this is what makes me happy that I should do it... I realized I wasn't happy. Nothing was making me happy, because you weren't beside me in my life."

At her words, his breath caught in his throat. He thought she was here to explain why she'd called things off. Never had he thought she was here to make things right.

"What are you saying?"

"I'm saying that I was wrong for thinking I couldn't give you what you deserved. I was wrong to be afraid. Because you've given me everything. You've never lied to me, you've always been open and honest, and everything you tell me is the truth whether I want to hear it or not. And while I was with you, you made me better. Stronger. Braver." She drew a deep breath. "You, Kane Harmon, make me feel fearless for the first time in my life. And I was too hurt by my mother to see that." She continued twisting her hands together in her lap, but her gaze never left his. "I love you and I want another chance," she whispered.

Holy fuck. He was out of his seat and pulling her into his arms in an instant. He breathed her in, squeezing her hard against him, afraid this was a dream or that she'd run again.

"You're here," he said, so damned relieved.

"Yes." She grinned.

"You're mine."

She nodded, falling into his chest.

"Say it."

She glanced up, bracing her hands on either side of his face, and looked into his eyes. "I'm yours and I'm not going anywhere."

He expelled a long stream of air. Okay. He could breathe now, maybe for the first time since that day outside his garage when he'd believed she'd walked out of his life for good.

He sealed his lips over hers, kissing her long and hard, not coming up for air. Not wanting to or needing to. Not when he finally had her back. He glided his tongue over her lips and slipped inside, groaning at the feel of coming home.

Unable to wait another minute, he picked her up and carried her into his bedroom, laying her down on the bed. He untied the top of the dress and let it fall down to her sides, then easily pulled the rest of the garment down and off, taking her underwear along with it.

She watched him with eager eyes and he couldn't wait, either. He undressed quickly and knelt over her, his gaze never leaving hers.

"I missed you," she said, tears shimmering in her eyes.

"I missed you, too, beautiful." He clasped her hands in his and slid into her, letting out a harsh groan at the feel of her tight, wet heat clenching around him.

"Say it," he said, needing to hear it now, while they were as close as two people could be.

"I'm yours," she promised, and he went on to claim her in the most primal of ways.

Afterwards, she lay in his arms, her fingers trailing over the hair on his chest. "I'm sorry," she said again.

"Don't." He shook his head. He didn't want to rehash the past. "If you needed to go through that to get us here, it's worth it in the end." Although he never wanted to feel her loss again.

She lay her head in the crook of his arm and sighed.

"You're braver than you think," he told her.

She laughed at that. "I'm going to get there and do you want to know why?"

"Of course."

She pushed herself up and looked into his eyes. "I'm no longer afraid, because you taught me how to live. You make me want to be fearless."

He laughed and tumbled her onto her back for another long kiss and he hoped the start of another round of lovemaking. Because everything he did with Halley was about love.

Epilogue

B Y THE END of September, Kane had completed Halley's deck and they decided to have a party to christen it. The ocean ebbed and flowed in the distance as the group gathered on the finished deck. Since Kane was all but living there when he wasn't working, they considered it their first joint party, small though the guest list was.

Halley had her family, Aunt Joy, Phoebe, and Jamie here, and Kane had his father, sister, and Nicky. Jamie and Nicky hit it off despite the age difference, Jamie at eleven and Nicky at seven years old, and headed off to hang out on the far corner of the large deck.

Jackson Traynor from Kane's garage arrived, carrying a six-pack of beer. He seemed happy to be here and was talking to Aunt Joy, Andi, and Phoebe about real estate prices in town.

And Monty was running from person to person,

jumping up on his hind legs and begging to be petted.

She'd never heard from her mother again… and she was grateful not to have to deal with her, but she'd minimized the damage the woman had caused. Halley had canceled the check and, at her aunt's urging, hired a private investigator to scour pawn shops to find the ring. He'd done it, returning the family heirloom to Halley last month.

Kane strode over and wrapped an arm around Halley's shoulders.

She sighed happily and leaned into him. "This is nice," she murmured.

"Agreed. So what's your sister's story? Think she'd be interested in Jackson?" he asked.

Halley shook her head. "Phoebe seems like she has herself together, but she's still sad about not being able to locate Jamie's dad. She got pregnant while in foster care and they were separated after. I think she just wants to focus on raising her son."

"Hmm. She's too big a personality to be alone forever, though," Kane said.

Halley shrugged. "I hope you're right. I want her to have what we've found." Standing up on her tiptoes, she kissed him on the lips.

"Mmm." He hooked an arm around her waist and pulled her flush against him. His cock pressed insistently against her stomach, making her almost wish they didn't have company.

"Hey, break it up. There are kids around," Phoebe called from across the deck.

Halley rolled her eyes at her sister. No one was a bigger Kane fan than Phoebe... except, of course, for Halley.

"I love you," she whispered.

"Love you, too, beautiful."

She blushed, but God, she'd never get tired of hearing him call her that. She patted his cheek. "Ready to break out the grill?" she asked.

"Can't wait."

"I'll go take orders," she said, heading over to the group of people she loved.

She knew how lucky she was, that Kane had taken her back and that she had this warm, loving group of people as her support system.

And she would never take family or Kane for granted again.

Next up in the Rosewood Bay series—Phoebe's story.

READ ON for a teaser of BREATHE.

ORDER your copy of BREATHE today.

BREATHE

Fall in love with the Wards

From troubled teen to successful general contractor, Jake Nichols changed his name and turned his life around. He's single and likes it that way, enabling him to focus on his job and occasional one night stands. On his agenda, a new project, one that could provide entry to a higher end clientele. All he needs is the okay of the realtor in charge. Little does he know his potential new business partner is a woman he once loved. And Jake is about to find more than just a job. He's about to discover he's a father.

Phoebe Ward has survived and conquered a painful past that includes foster care and becoming a teenaged mom. She wants nothing more than to focus on the present but it's hard when she looks into the eyes of her son, knowing she's tried and failed to find his father. She's resigned herself to raising him alone with the help of her family... Until a client meeting brings her face to face with her first love. A boy... now a sexy man she thought she'd never see again.

They knew each other as teenagers and now they have the chance to put the past behind them, forge a family, a future... and find love.

Order BREATHE today.

Chapter One

"JAMIE, GET DOWNSTAIRS for breakfast or you'll be late for school!" Phoebe Ward called for her son to come to the kitchen. By her calculation, they had fifteen minutes for breakfast and then they needed to get into the car for the drive to school.

"I'm here!" He skidded into the room wearing a navy hooded sweatshirt and a pair of black track pants and sneakers, smelling like he'd bathed in Axe. The strong, sharp scent, a combination of citrus and peppermint, was pungent and immediately destroyed her nasal passages and killed her appetite.

She breathed in through her mouth. "What did I say about overdoing the Axe before school?"

He looked at her with innocent eyes. "I didn't. You said I had to shower so I did."

And he'd bathed in the body wash and topped it off with deodorant. Nice. His teacher was going to have one hell of a migraine if every eleven-year-old in the room smelled the same way.

"I smell like a man," he said with a cheeky grin.

She bit back a laugh. "You smell like something,"

she muttered. "Eat your eggs. We need to get moving. I have an early appointment today."

He slid into his chair and began shoveling his food into his mouth. "Are you selling a house today?" he asked, glancing at her work suit that she wore for days she was meeting with clients.

"Chew and swallow before talking," she said. "First, I'm meeting a new contractor at Celeste's place," she said of her good friend who'd moved to the city. "She wants to sell the estate and I'm overseeing the renovations. Then I'm showing a listing this afternoon." She'd never worked with Masters Construction before, but according to Celeste, they'd won the bidding and came with solid references.

"Cool." He took two big bites of toast and gulped down his orange juice. "Done." He wiped his mouth on his sleeve and she sighed.

"You're finished. Chickens get done in the oven. Get your backpack together and let's get moving."

He picked up his plate, brought it to the sink, rinsed it off and stuck it in the dishwasher. He was a boy with all the quirky habits that came along with that, but he was a good kid. And considering she'd had him when she'd been sixteen and had been a single parent after that, with only her Aunt Joy and her sister Halley for backup, she was damned lucky they'd both turned out okay.

She smiled as he rushed around, repacking the bag that he should have put together the night before. "Slow down and make sure you have everything."

"I do. I'm ready."

She gathered her keys, deciding she'd pick up coffee on her way, and they headed out the door.

She dropped Jamie off at school and waved goodbye, watching until he walked safely inside. Afterwards, she stopped at Grace's Coffee Shop for a large vanilla latte, which she finished on the way over to Celeste's home, a large estate that would sell for a hefty price once renovated. She pulled into the driveway where a large Ford F-150 was already parked. The driver wasn't there so she exited her vehicle.

She had the house key, but she didn't need to let herself in. The door was open a crack and she toed it the rest of the way with her foot, walking in and shutting the door behind her.

"Hello?" She called out.

"In here!" a masculine voice said, sounding like it came from the far side of the house.

She followed the sound and caught sight of a man talking on the phone, his back to her. He was tall, well built, muscles defined, as she took him in from behind. And what a behind he had, a tight ass in his faded jeans.

She ogled the sight shamelessly, her gaze traveling

up his lean waist and broad shoulders. His dark hair was short and a jet black color she preferred on a man. Wearing a light blue button down, the sleeves were rolled up, revealing sexy forearms.

And then he turned to meet her gaze, giving her one raised finger to indicate he needed another minute on the phone. Except she wasn't paying attention to the gesture because one look at that handsome face, more mature than she remembered but just as good looking, and she froze.

Vivid blue eyes widened at the sight of her in return.

She wasn't just looking at a stranger, she was staring into the shocked eyes of her son's father, a man she hadn't seen since before she found out she was pregnant.

Order BREATHE today.

About the Author

Carly Phillips is the *N.Y. Times* and *USA Today* Best-selling Author of over 50 sexy contemporary romance novels featuring hot men, strong women and the emotionally compelling stories her readers have come to expect and love. Carly's career spans over a decade and a half with various New York publishing houses, and she is now an Indie author who runs her own business and loves every exciting minute of her publishing journey. Carly is happily married to her college sweetheart, the mother of two nearly adult daughters and three crazy dogs (two wheaten terriers and one mutant Havanese) who star on her Facebook Fan Page and website. Carly loves social media and is always around to interact with her readers.

Keep up with Carly and her upcoming books:

Website:
www.carlyphillips.com

Sign up for Carly's Newsletter:
www.carlyphillips.com/newsletter-sign-up

Carly on Facebook:
facebook.com/CarlyPhillipsFanPage

Carly on Twitter:
twitter.com/carlyphillips

Hang out at Carly's Corner! (Hot guys & giveaways!)
smarturl.it/CarlysCornerFB

87779190R00141

Made in the USA
Lexington, KY
30 April 2018